MICKEY SPILLANE

is back with three stories never before published in book form!

ME, HOOD!
which introduces Ryan, Spillane's toughest character yet.

"KICK IT OR KILL!"
When the fat man got through with the girl, she was never the same. Then came Kelly Smith, a tough guy with a hole in his side and vengeance in his heart. . . .

THE AFFAIR WITH THE DRAGON LADY
Here's a new and surprising Spillane, writing about the strangest affair you ever heard of!

Also by MICKEY SPILLANE

VENGEANCE IS MINE
MY GUN IS QUICK
THE BIG KILL
ONE LONELY NIGHT
THE SNAKE
KISS ME, DEADLY
THE GIRL HUNTERS
THE DEEP
I, THE JURY
THE LONG WAIT
KILLER MINE
THE FLIER
RETURN OF THE HOOD
DAY OF THE GUNS
BLOODY SUNRISE
THE DEATH DEALERS

and published by CORGI BOOKS

MICKEY SPILLANE

ME, HOOD!

CORGI BOOKS
A DIVISION OF TRANSWORLD PUBLISHERS

ME, HOOD!
A CORGI BOOK

First publication in book form
in Great Britain

Corgi Edition published 1963
Corgi Edition reprinted 1963
Corgi Edition reprinted 1964
Corgi Edition reissued 1967

Copyright, ©, Transworld Publishers Ltd., 1963

Corgi Books are published by Transworld Publishers Ltd.,
Bashley Road, London, N.W.10

Made and printed in Great Britain by
Richard Clay (The Chaucer Press), Ltd., Bungay Suffolk

CONTENTS

ME, HOOD!

ME, HOOD!

THEY picked me up in a bar on Second Avenue and waited for the supper crowd to flow out before they made their tap, two tall smiling lads with late model narrow-brim Kellys that helped them blend into the background of young junior executives.

But both of them had that almost imperceptible cock to their arms that comes from wearing a gun too long on one side, and that made them something else again.

When they came in they pulled out stools on either side of me and began the routine, but I saved them all the trouble they had planned to go to. I finished my drink, pocketed my change and stood up. "We go now?"

Without changing the size of his smile the one with the pale blue eyes said, "We go now."

I grinned, nodded toward the bartender and walked to the door. On the street a gentle nudge edged me north, then another turned me at the corner to where the car was parked. One got behind the wheel and one was on my right. I didn't feel any gun rubbing against my hip where it should have, so I knew the guy on my right had it in his hand.

At the door the squat little man stood with his legs spraddled and hands in his pockets, looking at nothing, yet watching everything. The other one sat on the window ledge at my shoulder without saying anything.

Across the city the clock on the square boomed nine. Behind me the door to the inside office opened and a voice said, "Bring him in."

Smiling Boy let me go ahead of him, followed me in and closed the door.

Then, for the first time, I was wishing I hadn't played the wise guy. I felt like an idiot for being so damn dumb and while I was trying to put it together I could feel the coldness creeping over me like a winter fog. I shut my mouth and grinned so I wouldn't start sounding off and let them see the hate I wore like my own skin.

Cops. Out of uniform, but cops. Five in front, one behind me. Two more in the room outside. There was something different about the five, though. The mold was the same, but the metal seemed tempered. If there were any cutting edges they were well hidden, yet ready to expose themselves as fast as a switch blade.

Five men in various shades of single-breasted blues and greys

9

with solemn dark ties on white that hinted at formality not found in general police work. Five pairs of expressionless, yet scrutinizing eyes that somehow seemed weathered and not too easily amused.

But the thin one at the end of the table was different, and I watched him deliberately and knew he was hating my guts just as hard as I was hating his.

From his place at the door, Smiling Boy said, "He knew us. He was waiting for us."

The thin one's voice had a flat quality to it. "You think much for . . . a punk."

"I'm not the kind of punk you're used to."

"How long have you known?"

I shrugged. "Since you started." I told him, "Two weeks."

They looked at each other, annoyed, some angry. One leaned forward on the desk, his face flushed. "How did you know?"

"I told you. I'm no ordinary punk."

". . . I asked you a question."

I looked at the guy at the table. His hands were tight and white at the knuckles, but his face had lost its flush. "I've been a while at this game myself," I said. "Every animal knows it's got a tail no matter how short it is. I knew I had mine the first day you tacked it on."

The guy looked past me to Smiling Boy. "Did you know that?"

My buddy at the door fidgeted a second, then: "No, sir."

"Was it ever suspected?"

Another hesitation. "No, sir. None of the reports from the other shifts mentioned it."

"Great," the man said, "just great." Then he looked back at me again. "You could have shaken this tail?"

"Anytime."

"I see." He paused and sucked his lip into his teeth. "But you preferred not to. Why?"

"Let's say I was curious."

"You have that kind of curiosity about someone who could be there to kill you?"

"Sure," I said. "I'm a foolish man. You know that."

"Watch your mouth, feller."

I grinned at him so hard that the scar across my back got tight. "Go to hell!"

"Listen . . ."

"No, you listen, you stinking, miserable little slob . . . don't tell me to watch my mouth. Don't tell me one lousy little thing to do at all or I'll tell you where to shove it. Don't try to peg me because I have a record. . . ."

In back of me the tall boy stopped smiling and hissed, "Let him say it out."

"Damn right, let me say it out. You got no choice. You're not fooling with a parolee or a hooker who's scared stiff of cops. I hate cops in general and right now you slobs in particular. This little shake has all the earmarks of a frame and brother, you're going in over your head if you try it."

"That all?"

"No," I said. "Now I'm done playing. I went along for the ride to see what the bit was and it stinks. So I leave. If you think I can't, then put the arm on me and try stopping me. Then you monkeys are going to have a pretty time trying to explain this set up to a couple of tabloids I got friends on."

The thin one said, "Finished?"

"Yeah. Now I'm leaving."

"Don't go."

I stopped and stared at him. Nobody had moved to get in my way at all. There was something tight about the way they all stood there, something all wrong about the play that I couldn't make. I could feel my back going tight again and I said, "What?"

The thin one swung around in his chair. "I thought you said you were a curious person."

I went back to the table. "Okay, friend. But before I get suckered in, answer me some questions."

The thin one nodded, his face impassive.

"You're cops."

He nodded, but now there was something new in his eyes. "All right, I'll qualify it. We're cops . . . of a sort."

I asked, "Who am I?"

His answer was flat and methodical. "Ryan. The Irish One. Sixteen arrests, one conviction for assault and battery. Suspected of being involved in several killings, several robberies and an uncooperative witness in three homicide cases. Associates with known criminals, has no visible source of income except for partial disability pension from World War II. Present address . . ."

"That's enough," I said.

He paused and leaned back. "Also—you're rather astute."

"Thanks. I went to college for two years."

"It made a difference criminally?"

"It made no difference one way or another. Get on with the pitch."

His fingers made a slow roll on the table top.

"You knew you had been tailed for two weeks. Do you know why?"

"First guess is that you're figuring a fix for me to turn stoolie," I said. "If that's it you've wasted time because you aren't that smart to catch me off base."

II

"Then you think you're smarter than an entire law enforcement agency?"

They watched me. Nobody said a thing.

Finally I said, "Okay. I'm a curious guy. Spell it out slow in punk language so I won't miss the juicy parts."

The others left the room when the thin one nodded.

He said, "There is a job that must be done. We can't do it because of several factors involved. One is simple enough to understand; it is possible . . . even probable that we are known to those of . . . the opposition forces. The other reason has a psychological factor involved."

"It must be a beauty," I said.

He went on as if he had never heard me. "Our groups are highly skilled. Although those chosen to augment our group are of the finest calibre, the most select, elite . . . they still have certain handicaps civilized society has inflicted on them. Maybe you can finish it for me."

I nodded. "Sure. Let's try a lucky guess. You need an animal. Some improver of the breed has run all shagginess out of your business-suit characters and you need a downtown shill to bait your hook. How close did I come?"

"Close," he said.

"I'm still listening."

"We need somebody of known talents. Like you. Somebody whose mind can deal on an exact level with . . . the opposition. We need someone whose criminal disposition can be directed into certain channels."

"An animal," I said, "the dirty kind. Maybe a jackal that can play around in the jungle with the big ones without being caught."

"It's descriptive enough."

"Not quite. The rest of it is that if he's killed he wouldn't even be missed or counted for a loss."

When he answered, he said, "That isn't exactly '*punk language*'."

"But I'm there, huh?"

"You're there," he said solemnly.

I shook my head slowly. "*Brother!*" I pushed away from the desk and straightened up. "I think you made a mistake in nomenclature, buddy. It's not a psychological factor involved, it's a philosophical one. Only your appeal is psychological. You posed me a pretty, laddie."

"I . . . don't suppose it would do much good to appeal on a patriotic basis?"

"You suppose right. You can shove flag-waving and duty-to-your country crap with the rest of it."

"Then how do I appeal?"

"To curiosity and one thing more. Money!"

"How much?"

I grinned real big, all the way across my face. "A bundle, friend. For what you want, a bundle. Tax-free, no strings, in small, used bills."

"What is it that I wanted?" he asked.

For fun I played it straight. I said, "You clued me, friend. Patriotism doesn't exist on any local level. Suddenly we're international and I can only think of three fields where you striped pantsers could exploit me. The narcotic trade through Italy, Mexico or China; illegal gold shipments to Europe; then last, the Commies."

He didn't answer.

"How much?" I asked.

"You can get your bundle."

"Like I said? Tax free, small bills . . ."

"Like you said," he repeated.

"One more point."

"Ask it," he told me.

"What makes you think I'll like the bit?"

"Because you hate cops and politicians and those are the kind of people you'll get a chance to really crack down on."

I squinted at him. "You're leaving something out."

"You're right, Irish. You're communicating now, boy. I left out the needle. Money is a powerful motivator, but the needle still has to be there. If you take the deal we supply the *toxin-anti-toxin*."

"So?"

"You'll take it?"

I nodded. "Sure. What'd you expect me to say?"

"Nothing." With his fingers he drew a paper from his pocket, unfolded it so the bottom showed with the signature line and nothing more, then he passed me his pen. "Sign it."

The laugh came out of me of its own accord. Why ask to read it? I had nothing I could sign away and nothing to confess to that couldn't be broken in court and nothing makes me more curious than signing first and asking to read later. I signed.

I said, "What's the pitch?"

"Nothing you'd appreciate. To protect ourselves or yourself under impossibly remote circumstances you now have a certain measure of legal protection."

"Like what?"

"Like you were just made a cop," he said.

I took it easy and said all the words slowly and plainly so he wouldn't miss a one and after a long time I ran out. His face had turned white and the corners of his mouth were pulled back tight.

13

"You finished?" he said.

"It's all the punk language I can think of right now."

"I don't like the arrangement any better than you do. It's a necessity or it never would have happened. You're in."

"Suppose I crap out?"

"You won't."

"Okay, I asked for it. Now what do you do, indoctrinate me or something?"

"Not at all. All you're going to do is be given a name. You'll find that person. Then whatever is necessary to do . . . you do."

"Damn, man, can't you make sense?"

The smile came back again. "Making sense of it is your job. The picture will come clear by itself. You'll know what to do."

"Sure. Great." I asked the question. "Who?"

"The name is Lodo."

"That's all?"

He nodded. "That's all. Just find him. You'll know what to do."

"Then the loot?"

"A big bundle of it. More than you've ever had in your life."

"How long do I have?"

"No time limit."

I let the laugh out easily. His eyes tightened when the laugh spread to my face. "Just for the record before we turn the machine off, friend . . . who steered you to me?"

"A man named Billings. Henry Billings. Familiar?"

Something choked the laugh off in my throat. "Yeah, I know him."

Know him? The lousy slob ratted on me to the M.P.'s about liberating 10 grand of some kraut's gold hoard back in '45 and while I was getting the guardhouse treatment when some planted coins were found in my footlocker, he walked off with the stuff himself. The day I caught up with him would be his last.

When I knew nothing was showing on my face I said, "Where could I find him?"

"Out in Brooklyn . . . in a cemetery."

I felt like kicking the walls out of the building. I had nursed that hate for too long to have it snatched away from me like that. *Thirteen years now I had been waiting.*

"What happened?"

"He was shot."

"Yeah?"

"He was after the same name."

I said, "Yeah?" again.

"Before he died he recommended you. He said you were the only one he knew who was a biggard bastard than he was himself."

"He was lying."

"You still with it?"

"Sure." *I wouldn't miss it for anything now. Someplace Billings had bought something with that 10 G's and whatever he got was mine now no matter who I had to take it away from.* "Where do I start?"

"With a phone number. Billings had it on him."

"Whose?" I said.

"You find out. We couldn't figure it."

Once again he dipped into his pocket. He came up with a pad and wrote a phone number on it, a Murray Hill exchange. He let me see it, then tore it out and held a match under it.

Outside, I whistled up a cab and cruised back toward the main stem, trying hard to think my way out of the situation. It had all the earmarks of a sucker trap and somehow I got elected to try it out. Me, strictly Brooklyn Irish, old Ryan himself, heading straight for the plastic pottie boobie prize.

Man, I thought, I'm not new to this business. I've been around a long while and made plenty the easy way without pulling time. Even the hard boys on the big team uptown stayed off my back.

At 49th St. and Sixth Ave. I paid off the cabbie and walked to Joe DiNuccio's. I went into the back room where I knew Art Shay would be and slid in across the booth from him.

Art's a funny guy. He does feature writing for a syndicated outfit, but he could have been a great reporter or TV analyst if something hadn't happened between him and some broad before he got back from Germany in '45. Now he was spending all his time on assignments, working hard to get himself killed.

His eyes peered at me over the top of the galley proofs he was checking. "What're you crawling after now?"

I grinned at him. "Something funny's happening to me."

"That shouldn't be a new feeling for you, Ryan. Who's bump list you on now?"

"Art," I said. "Tell me something. Have you ever known the fuzz to use a hood for anything except a stoolie?"

The corners of his eyes stretched taut. "No. Not the straight boys, anyway. What have you got going?"

"Nothing special. I'm just curious about a few things."

"Any story in it?"

"Maybe."

"Want to talk about it?"

"Not yet. Things aren't squared away. Maybe you can fit in some pieces. Ever hear of a man named Billings?"

His eyes opened a little wider. "Same one who got gunned down a few days ago?"

I nodded.

"It was just a squib in the paper. Called a gang killing." He stopped suddenly and looked at me hard. "Ryan . . . I remember ten years back when you were talking about killing a guy by that name. Did you tap him?"

"I didn't have the luck, kiddo. That tap was somebody else's."

"The conversation is fascinating, Ryan. Keep it up."

"Okay, read this. Billings wasn't a small tap at all. That guy had something so big it would have made front page for a week."

"Like what?"

I shook my head. "I'm new to it too."

"How are you involved?"

"Because Billings had something he knew could get me killed too. It was the last thing he ever did, but he did it good. That warped slob had to live like a snake just to stay alive ever since he framed me and he made up for it, all right." I stopped and grinned real big. "At least he thought he did."

Art dropped his chin in his hand and nodded. "What can I do?"

"As an accredited reporter, you can get some official answers. Get any statement Billings made and any details on how he was killed. Can do?"

"Shouldn't be hard. Those reports are on file." He waited a moment, then said, "You're giving me a small worm for a big hook."

"Thanks." I uncurled myself and got up. "Ever know anyone called Lodo?"

He thought a moment, then shook his head. "Nothing there. Important?"

"Who knows. Think on it."

"Sure. Where can I reach you?"

"Remember Papa Manny's old three-floor brownstone?"

"Off Second?"

"I own it now. I live in the basement apartment."

The Murray Hill exchange the thin one had given me wasn't a phone. It was a coded password that got you admission into a horse parlor operating right on Broadway. It wasn't one of the things the cops could be expected to know, not even the grafters.

But I knew. I even had the latest job. The one they gave me was three weeks old. The boy on the door winked, said, "Hi, Ryan, come in an' spend a buck."

The place had changed some. The loot was flowing in. The board was bigger, there was free booze at a service bar and fat chairs where the benches used to be.

Jake McGaffney came out from behind the pay window, saw me and came over. "Changing rackets, kid?"

16

"Not me, Jake. I like mine better. They got to be sure things for me."

"We got a few of those too," he chuckled. "What's on your mind?"

I nudged his arm and steered him to the end of the pay window. "You getting touched by anybody?"

"You know this operation, Ryan. We're not paying off. Hell, the cops know we're operating, but we move too fast for them to line us up."

"Nobody trying to cut in?"

"Get with it, boy. Since I played ball at the trial, uptown lets me go my own way. Sure, they give me limits and it's okay with me. Nobody's shaking me though. What's got you?"

"Did you know Billings?"

"Sure. He got gunned." Then he stopped and his face looked drawn. "He didn't leave any tracks to this place, did he?"

"Nothing that can tie in. The fuzz had an old MU code he wrote down."

Jake let his face relax and picked a butt from his pack and lit it. Through the smoke he said, "I'm okay then. They would've hit me before this if they figured it."

"Jake . . . got any idea why Billings got tapped?"

"Idea?" He laughed in his chest. "Hell, man, I *know why*."

"Why, Jake?"

"He had twelve thousand skins in his pocket when he left here. A nag called *Annie's Foot* came in and he was riding it hard."

"He been coming here long?"

"A month, maybe. I got a memo on him from his first play if you want it."

"Who steered him in?"

"Gonzales. You know little Juan Gonzales . . . he's the one pulled that kid outa the Hudson River sometime back and got his picture in the tabs. He was down the docks goofing off when this lady starts to scream and . . ."

"Where is he now, Jake?"

"Gonzales?" he seemed surprised. "He got killed three weeks ago. He got loaded and stepped right out in front of a truck. He got dead quick. No waiting around."

I said, "He have a family?"

"Just some dame. You wait . . . I'll get you the business."

He went behind the window and poked around in a card file until he found what he wanted. It was a short history of Juan Gonzales and when I memorized the data I handed it back. "Keep it if you want," he said.

"I don't need it."

Juan Gonzales had lived on 54th, a few houses down from

Tenth Ave. It was a fringe area where total integration of the underprivileged of all classes fused into a hotbed of constant violence. Lucinda Gonzales had a second floor rear apartment. The bells never worked in these tenements so I just went up and knocked at the door. It opened on a chain and a pretty, dark face peered at me and queried, "Si . . . who is it?"

"Lucinda Gonzales?"

"Si."

"I want to speak about Juan. Can I come in?"

She hesitated, shrugged, then closed the door to unhook the chain. I stepped inside and she leaned back against the door.

"I can tell you are not the policeman."

"That's right."

"You are not one of Juan's friends, either."

"How do you know?"

"His friends are all peegs. Not even tough guys. Just peegs."

"Thanks."

"What you want?"

"I want to know about Juan. You married?"

She made a wry face. "Nothing by the church. But this is not what you want to say."

This time I gave her a little grin. "Okay, chicken . . . I'll put it this way . . . Juan got loaded and got himself killed. He . . ."

"He did?" the sarcasm was thick. I stopped and let her say the rest. "Juan did not drink, señor."

"What's bothering you, Lucinda?"

"You, señor." Her arms were folded tightly across her breasts, making them half rise from her dress. "To me you look like the one who could do it."

"Do what?"

"Make Juan go crazy with fear. Maybe chase him so he runs in front of the truck and gets killed. All this time I have waited because I knew soon that somebody would come. They would have to come here. There is no other place. Now you are here, señor, and I can kill you like I have been waiting to do."

She unfolded her arms. In one hand she had a snub-nose rod and at that distance there wasn't a chance she could miss me.

"You better be sure, chicken," I said.

Her voice was getting a hysterical calm. There was a dull happy look in her eyes that meant she was crowding the deep end and so was I. "I *am* sure, señor."

I said very deliberately, "How do you know?"

"I know those of who Juan would be afraid. You are such a one. You thought he had his money when he died. He did not. Those ten thousand dollars, señor . . . it was here."

"Ten thousand . . ." My voice was soft, but she heard it.

Her smile was vicious. "But it is not here now. It is safe. It is

18

in the bank and it is mine. For such a sum Juan died. Now you can follow him."

She took too long to shoot. She thought of Juan first and her eyes flooded at the wrong time. I slapped my hand over hers and the firing pin bit into my skin when I yanked the rod out of her hand. When she started to scream, I belted her across the mouth and knocked her into a chair. She tried another one and I back-handed it loose and as though I snapped my fingers, the glazed look left her eyes and she stared at me from a face contorted by fear.

When she had it long enough I said, "Ease off. You won't get hurt."

She didn't believe me. She had lived with one idea too long.

"Lucinda . . . I never knew Juan. I don't want his bundle. That clear?"

She nodded.

"Where'd the ten grand come from?"

Defiance showed across her face. Then it all came back again; fear, disbelief, hatred, defiance.

I said, "Listen to me, sugar. If I wanted to I could make you talk a real easy way. It wouldn't be hard. I could make you scream and talk and scream and talk and you couldn't stop it. You know this?"

She bobbed her head once, quickly.

"But I don't want anything that bad. I'm not going to do anything like that. Understand?"

"Si."

"Then once more . . . where'd the ten G's come from?"

Nervously, she ran her fingers through her hair. "He came home from the docks one day and told me that soon we would go back to the island. Only now it would not be a mud hut but in a fine building that we would live. He said we were going to have much money. We would travel around the world, maybe."

"When was this?"

"The week before he died, señor."

"He had it then?"

"No." She stood up quickly and stepped to the table, turned and leaned back against it. "He was *getting* it then," he said. He was feeling very good. But he did not drink."

She shrugged. "He changed. He became a scared one. He would tell me nothing. Nothing at all. The same night he . . . died . . ." she paused and put her face in her hands a moment before going on, ". . . . he came in and took something from where he hid it in the closet."

"What was it?"

"I do not know. It was not very big. I theenk it could have been a gun. One time he kept a gun there wrapped up in rags.

19

He did not show me. He went out for maybe an hour. When he came back he had this money. He gave it to me and told me to pack up. Then he left."

"Where to?"

"To die somewhere, señor. He said he was going to . . . how you say it . . . arrange things."

"You have the dough."

"Is it really mine?"

I flipped the rod in my hand then tossed it on top of the table. "Sure it's yours," I told her. "Why not?"

She picked up the gun, studied it and laid it down again. "I am sorry if I . . . almost shot you."

"You could have been sorrier. You could have gotten your picture in the morning papers real easy."

Her smile was grim. "Yes. Like Juan." She opened a drawer in the dish closet and took out two front pages from recent tabloids and handed them to me. In one Juan was a hero. In the other he was dead.

But on his last public appearance there was an out-of-character bit for what I had been thinking. The truck driver who killed him was sitting on the curb crying.

I reached for the door. Before I opened it I said, "Did Juan ever mention a man named Lodo?"

"Lodo? Si. Twice he says this name. It was when he was very scared."

I let go the door, all edgy again. "Who is he?"

"He was asleep when he said this name, señor. I do not know. I do not ask, either."

I closed the door quietly behind me and went back downstairs. It had started to rain and the street stank.

The truck that had killed Juan was one of the Abart fleet from Brooklyn. I told the harried little boss I was an insurance investigator and he told me I had 20 minutes before Harry Peeler would be in and to have a seat.

At 5:40 a short thin guy with grey hair came in and the girl there said, "That gentleman's waiting to see you, Harry. Insurance investigator."

"It's about the . . . accident, I suppose."

"Well, yes."

"Terrible." He glanced at me ruefully. "I'm finished driving, Mr. Ryan. I can't go it any more."

"I want you to tell me about that night."

"But I told . . ."

"You've had a chance to think it over since then, Mr. Peeler. You've gone over every detail a thousand times, haven't you?"

He moaned, "Oh, help me, yes. Yes, every night. I can't forget it."

"Tell me about it, Mr. Peeler."

"How can I explain something crazy like that? It was three
A.M. and nobody was on the streets. I was driving toward the
bridge when this guy comes from in front of this parked truck.
Right under the wheels!"

"Was he running?"

At first he didn't answer. When he looked up, he had a puzzled
expression working at his face, then he said, "He kind of flew."

"What?"

"I know it sounds crazy, but that's what it was like. He must
have been standing there all along, just waiting. He didn't run.
He dove, like. You know what I mean. Maybe he was commit-
ing suicide. He dove, like."

"Could he have been pushed, like?"

Harry Peeler's eyes opened wide, startled. He swallowed hard,
thinking. "He . . . could have been."

"You've been thinking that, haven't you?"

He swallowed again.

I said, "It wasn't your fault. You couldn't have done anything
to prevent it."

He wasn't looking at me. He was squinting at the far wall and
I heard him say, "Somebody ran from behind that truck. I know
it. It took a while to remember, but I know it! I was yelling for
somebody to get a doctor. It was a long while before anybody
came. Somebody was behind that truck, though."

I stood up and patted his shoulder. "Okay. You feel better
now?"

"Sure." He grinned. "It ain't good to kill somebody, but it's
better knowing you couldn't of stopped it anyhow."

"That's the way. You keep driving."

I made a double check around Harry Peeler's neighborhood.
He was a long time resident and strictly a family man. Everybody
liked the guy. When I got done asking questions, I was pretty
sure of one thing.

Harry Peeler hadn't been in on any killing except by co-
ncidence.

The rain had started again, driving the city indoors. DiNuccio's
was crowded and smelled of beer and damp clothes. Art was
waiting for me, in the back. When I sat down, I said, "Let's
have it."

"Sure. Killed with a .38 slug in the chest, two in the stomach.
Now here's an item the papers didn't have. He wasn't shot
where he died. My guess is that he was thrown from a car. The
officers on the scene first aren't talking so it's my guess again that
he talked before he kicked off. Item two: I ran into so many icy

stares when I pushed this thing that I got the idea somethi
pretty hot was being covered up. A check through a good frie
came up with this bit . . . there's some kind of a grumble d
where the high hoods sit."

"What else on Billings?"

"Briefly, his last address was a midtown hotel and the name
phony. He was traced back through two others, but no further

"Source of income?"

"His latest room had an assortment of bum dice and new-bu
marked decks of cards very cleverly packaged and stamped. I
was a sharpie. A few receipted bills and match covers placed hi
working cheap places around here and in Jersey."

"Ten years," I said. "All that time under my nose and I nev
got near him."

"Be happy, chum." He flipped his pages over and scanne
them, picking out pieces of information. "One thing more.
found a couple of shills he played with before he died. He wa
talking about having a roll waiting. He was going into big tim
Nobody paid any attention to him right then."

I thought a moment, remembering how Billings operated i
the Army. "Was he flush when he played?"

"Those shills said he always had enough risk capital to entic
some nice fat bankrolls." He looked at me and put his note
away. "Now let's hear what you have to say," he said softly.

I shook my head at him. "This is stupid. Everything
doubling back. It starts and ends too fast. You sure you go
everything on Billings?"

"Yeah." I waved the waiter over for a beer and then knocke
half of it off in a long pull. "I'm going to guess a little bit here
but see how it works out.

"Billings was a funny guy. He used to say he'd wait for th
big one to come along if he waited all his life. He foxed me out o
ten grand in the army and when I got out of the guardhous
he'd been discharged. He hung onto that roll and used it a
sucker bait for his rigged games. I doubt if he took anybody fo
too much. That would have spoiled it. Those games were listen
ing posts waiting for that big one. All he'd bother to make woul
be living expenses.

"Then a guy named Juan Gonzales, who was a small tim
pay-off man for a friend of mine, must have sat in, saw the ro
and talked up horses. He even got Billings passed into the rooms
Matter of fact, the night he was killed he had twelve G's on him."

Art let out a slow whistle. "He was clean when he was found."

"Nobody would let that lay around, kiddo. It could have bee
a motive for his death."

"For twelve G's he could get a firstclass ride in this town, no
just a plain mugging."

I said, "Now listen . . . this Juan Gonzales had been killed a couple weeks earlier. Before he got it he was talking big money to his common-law wife, then he got scared spitless for some reason, showed up with ten grand, handed it to her and went out and got bumped."

"I remember the case. Front page. He had just . . ."

"That's the guy."

"In other words, your point is that in either case the motive could possibly be robbery."

"Yeah, only it isn't. First because I'm in and next because there's a lid on the deal. It's real stupid. Everything doubles back. You sure you have everything on Billings?"

"He was buried at the city's expense and the only bunch of flowers came from the *Lazy Dazy Flower Shop*. The graveyard attendant remembered the name. If you want him exhumed, dig him up yourself."

"Sure." I threw a buck on the table. "Keep in touch."

My watch said 9:55 and I was tired. I found a cab outside, got off at my corner and started up toward my apartment.

The first pitch came from Pete-the-Dog who sold papers with a broken-throated growl. It came again from Mamie Huggins who waited until I passed by to put out her garbage and it came again by low whistle from the shadows across the street.

Two of them. Unknowns. They were waiting in my apartment.

I came through the back way Papa Manny always used when the police raided the old love factory he ran. I picked up the .45 from the shelf, cocked it under my arm so the click of the hammer was inaudible and stood there in the dark until my eyes were used to it.

One stood looking out the window. The other sat right in front of me and he was the one I put the cold snout of the gun against. I said, "Be at ease, laddies. You move and you're dead."

I stepped inside and prodded my boy. He got up obediently and walked to the wall. The other one got the idea and did the same. They both leaned against it while I patted them down and waited while I flicked on the light. Then I dumped the shells from the *Cobras* they carried in belt holsters and laid them on an end table. They both were too mad to spit.

The guy from the window I knew. I had met him a few days ago up in that apartment far above the city. The other was a new face. That one looked at me coldly, then to the gun. "You have a license for that?"

I grinned at him. "Let's say a poetic one, cop. I signed a piece of paper up there the boss man says allows me certain liberties."

"There's only one copy and it can be torn up very easily."

"Not for a simple fracture like this, you slob. Now knock it

23

off. If you're so damn dumb you can't break and enter without being spotted you ought to join the fire department."

The other one said, "Lay off, Ryan."

"Okay," I said. "So let's hear what's going on and get out."

He hated me silently and then put on his blank face again. "To be simple about it, we'd like a progress report."

I said, "Nobody told me anything about this junket. I got sent off cold. What do you expect from me?"

"All right. What do you want to know?"

"How did you contact Billings?"

"We didn't. He came to us. He had something to sell."

"Like what?"

"We don't know. It was international in scope and big enough to cause a muss in this country. Our people overseas picked up information that there was trouble in high places. It was from there that we found out that Billings was a key figure."

"Somebody has quite an organization," I said.

"It's as big as ours."

"Go on."

"Billings apparently overplayed it. He wanted to sell what he had. We decided to go along. We assigned four men to keep him protected ... top men, I might add. They worked in teams of two and both teams were killed. Four good men, Ryan, highly trained, killed like rank amateurs. It was Billings who found the last team. He called and said he was getting out and that was when he told us about you.

"He got out, all right. He was as cute as you with a trick dodge. He didn't last very long, though. He caught it that night."

"Nothing was in the paper about those boys getting killed."

"That was easy enough to fix."

"Yeah." I walked across the room and pulled a cold beer from the cooler. "Tell me ... Billings wasn't dead when he was found. What did he say?"

I watched their faces. They couldn't help it, but their eyes touched, briefly.

"Okay, Ryan, you're sharp. He wasn't dead. He said it was Lodo. That's where we got the name. We have nothing else on it."

They didn't know and I didn't tell them that another dead man had known Lodo. How many more?

I said, "One more thing ... was any money found on Billings?"

His voice was a little too flat. "What do you mean?"

"The police reports say he was clean. It earmarked a robbery."

"So?"

"What happened to the twelve grand?"

My friend held his mouth tight. "How did you know about that?"

"I get around."

Before he could answer, it came to me. It was all backwards and wrong, but it could make sense to them. I said, "If you're thinking I sold him something for twelve grand, you're gone, man. You just loused your picture up. Now I'm reading you R5-S5. You pigs conned me into taking on a kill job with hopes of hanging me. All this while I had in the back of my mind I was doing something that could make you idiots look jerky and because you asked me to at that. In fact, a couple of times I caught myself enjoying doing something straight for a change. Brother, what a sucker I was!

"So my old buddy Billings tips you to me before he's found dead with twelve G's in his pocket. So I'm on the spot. Oh, man, this is crazy. What was I supposed to do . . . get so shook that I left a hole in my scheme somewhere that I'd try backtracking until I tripped myself up?"

I let go of the mad slowly, and when I had it down where it belonged, I grinned at them. "Laddies, you're devious thinkers, but you thunk wrong. I got you by the short hairs now. I'm in and you're out. I'm going to ride this one for all it's worth. I'm so far ahead of you right now it's pathetic and it'll stay that way. You tell the boss man to get that pile of small bills ready, y'hear?"

They didn't answer me.

"I want one more thing," I said. "I want a copy of my 'appointment' and a number where you guys can be reached sent to me care of General Delivery at 34th Street. I want a license for this gun and the number is 127569. Remember it. Now blow out of here and don't bother laying a tail on me. It won't work. If I want you I'll call and that's the only progress report you'll get."

You go up 16 floors and you get off in a plush foyer surrounded by antique furniture and a lovely redhead who smiles and you are encompassed by *Peter J. Haynes, III. Co., Inc.*

She looked up at me, button by button until she came to my eyes, then she stopped and smiled a little bit bigger. To her I was something different than the usual Haynes client even though mine was a $200 suit. The shirt was white and the collar spread. The tie was black knitted and neat and the cuffs that showed were the proper half inch below the coat cuff. The links were plain, but gold, and they showed. The only thing out of place was my face. I don't think I looked like the typical Haynes client. I wasn't carrying a briefcase, either. I was carrying a rod, but that was one reason for the $200 suit. It didn't show.

The redhead said, "Good morning."

I said, "Hello, honey."

She said, "Can I help you?"

I said, "Anytime."

She said, "Please . . ."

I said, "I should be the one to say please."

She said, "*Stop* it!"

I said, "What'll you give me if I do?"

Then she smiled and said, "You're crazy."

I smiled back, "Is Carmen Smith here?"

"It would have to be her," she said. "Yes, she's here. Is she expecting you?"

"No."

"Then you can't see her."

"Who's going to keep me out?" I said.

She got the grin back. "Nobody around here, I guess. Miss Smith is down the hall, at the end. She'll be mad."

"Tough."

She went down the buttons again in reverse. "I hope so. Stop by to say so-long."

I grinned at her. "I will, don't worry."

Miss Smith was encompassed by two girl secretaries and a queer. She was behind a desk talking into a hush-a-phone, doodling on an early *Times* edition. When I walked in, I waved a thumb at the dolls and they got out. The queer took longer until he looked straight at me. Miss Smith said something into the HP and hung up. Then she pushed back her chair and stood up.

Most times a woman is nothing. Sometimes you can classify them as pretty or not pretty. Sometimes you can say this one I like or this one I do not like.

Then one day you see one who is totally unlike all the rest and this is one you not only like but one you must have. This is one who has been waiting a long time for somebody and instinctively you know that until now she hasn't found that one. She's big and beautiful and stands square-shouldered like a man, but she's full-breasted and taut and completely undressed beneath the sheath she has on. She's not trying for anything. She doesn't have to. You don't have to look to know she's long-legged and round and in her loins there's a subtle fire that can be fanned, and fanned, and fanned.

I said the obvious. "Miss Smith?"

"Yes."

"My name is Ryan."

"I have no morning appointments."

"Now you have, kitten."

I let her take a good look at me. It didn't take long. She knew. I wasn't taking any apple out of her hand.

"Can I help you?"

"Sure, honey. That you can do."

"Well."

26

"A flower shop . . . the Lazy Dazy . . . in Brooklyn, tells me you sent a bouquet to a friend of mine."

It would be hard to describe the brief play that went across her face.

"Billings," I said. "He was killed. He got one bunch of flowers. Yours."

Again, it happened, that sympathetic sweep of emotions touching her eyes and her mouth. She sat down at an angle, woman-like, with her knees touching, and her hand on the desk shook a little.

"You . . . are a friend?"

"Not of his. Were you?"

Her eyes filled up and she made a motion with her head before reaching for the tissues in her drawer. "I'm sorry. I can never quite get used to people dying whom I know."

"Don't let it get you, sugar. He wasn't worth it."

"I know, but he was still someone I was familiar with. May I ask who you are?"

"The name is Ryan, honey. In common parlance I'm a hood. Not a big one, but I get along."

There was a silent appeal in her eyes. "I don't . . . quite . . ."

"Where do you come off knowing a bummer like Billings?"

"Why should I tell you?"

"Because if I don't get the answer, the cops will."

She sucked in her breath, filling the tanned skin of her bosom, swelling it against the dress.

I said, "How well did you know Billings?"

"Tell me something first. Since you seem so interested in me, have you . . . let's say . . . investigated me in any way?"

"Nope."

"Mr. Ryan . . . I'm a gambler."

"A good one?"

"One of the best. My father was a professional. According to his need or current morals, he would work it right or wrong. No better card mechanic ever lived. He supported me in style."

"You . . . ?"

"Mother died at my birth. My father never married again. He gave me everything including an education in mechanics to the point where I can clean a table any time I want to."

"This doesn't explain Billings."

"I'm a card player, Mr. Ryan. I'm in on all the big games that ever happen in this city. I win more than I could possibly make at a mundane job from fat little men who love to show off before a woman. If you're really a hood, then ask around the slap circuit who I am. I'm sure they'll be able to tell you."

"I don't have to ask. But that still doesn't explain Billings."

"Billings was a queer draw. He was a good mechanic at times, but not good enough to work against the big ones. Straight, he was all right. One day he sat in with us and I caught him working and cut him loose. He never did figure it until I got him invited again. You see, Mr. Ryan, these types are fun for me. I was able to chop him down to nothing just for the fun of it."

"How much did you take him for?"

"Just for hundreds. He had money, but we were playing for cards, understand? Money isn't quite that important."

"He was good?"

"Very. But just not that good."

"When did you see him last?"

She didn't hesitate. "Three days before he was killed."

"This you can prove?"

When she had her composure back, she said simply. "I should never have sent him flowers."

"That wasn't the bit, kid."

"No? What was then?"

"You're a big gal. A VP of a promising industry. You make fifteen hundred a week in your job and while the boss is away you're head doll here. You have a penthouse on Madison Avenue and charge accounts in the best stores. So you like to gamble. You like to play cards. This wasn't hard to find out at all."

"I thought you hadn't investigated me."

"I didn't. I picked it all up from one talkative building attendant."

"Then why are you considering me suspect, Mr. Ryan?" the tears were there.

"You sent him a five-dollar bouquet, kid."

And she didn't hesitate this time, either. "He was a five-dollar card player, Mr. Ryan."

"And you're sentimental?"

"No, but it was a gesture to the cheap dead."

"The gesture could be vindictive."

"When you're dead it doesn't matter. It was a gesture. Now I'm sorry for it."

"I don't like it, baby," I told her softly.

When she looked up, the VP was gone and I could have been looking at her across a table somewhere. She was all woman and coldly wild, with full-house eyes ready to sweat me out. It only lasted a second, but while it did I knew there was no bluff.

She said, "My father was well known at Monte Carlo. He was even better known at Vegas. His name wasn't Smith. One day he was shot by a crazy little man who lost his own roll with his own marked cards."

"What happened to the crazy little man?"

"The nine-year-old daughter of the dead man blew his head off with a shotgun from ten feet away."

28

I said quietly, "You?"

"Me."

"You sent *him* a five dollar bouquet too?"

"No." Her smile was clean and straight across. "The girl daddy was living with did, though."

"I like the gesture," I said coldly.

"I think it was fitting." Her tone matched mine.

"Now?"

"Something has come up as regards Mr. Billings. He was killed and now you're here. Not the police. Just you. Why?"

I said, "Billings left me to the dogs for ten grand one time. I think he did it again. I'm a little anxious to find out who's involved in this play."

"You think I might be one?"

"I don't know, but baby . . . I'm going to find out real soon."

"I'm not sorry he's dead," she said. "To me it doesn't matter one way or another. In a way, perhaps, I'm glad, nevertheless, I don't care. How you fit into this is no concern of mine. Is there anything else?"

I grinned and stood up and leaned over her desk. I said, "Yeah, kid, one thing more. Like you've been told a million times, you're an interesting wench. I wish you weren't out of it. From now on it's all going to be real dull."

Until now she hadn't smiled. When she did it was with a wet mouth and white teeth that made something happen no matter how early it was. She was hazel eyes, and suddenly chestnut hair, then even more quickly something slippery your hands should try to hold but couldn't.

She was big. Not as big as me, but big. When she uncurled and faced me she said, "No . . . I'll have to change it for you. Nobody ever called me that before."

"What before?"

"Merely interesting."

"My apologies."

"Not accepted here, Mr. Ryan." She looked at her watch, then smiled across at me. "It's almost noon. I'll let you apologize at lunch."

"It's getting cute again, kid."

Her smile had a question in it, then she understood what I meant. She laughed outright this time. "Let me put it this way, Mr. Ryan . . . there is a reason I want to be with you a little longer. You see, I've known many men . . . but I never had lunch with a real hood before. Shall we go?"

I took her to Pat Shane's for lunch. We ate on the dark side, in a back booth away from big ears and cigar smoke. By the time the steaks were gone, there was little I didn't know about Carmen Smith.

She reached across the table and laid her hand on top of mine. "Ryan . . . do you think you'll ever find out who killed Billings?"

I turned my hand over and held hers. "I'll find them."

"Is it . . . dangerous?"

That got a short laugh from me. "It's not exactly a soft touch. A couple of guys already died."

"A couple?"

"Just a detail. A little guy named Juan Gonzales. Ever hear of him?"

"No . . . it isn't familiar."

A second thought occurred to me. "Look, Carmen . . . When Billings was around you . . . was he ever scared?"

"The last time he was . . . well, nervous. He played pretty badly."

"Were the stakes big?"

"Very petty that time. We all kidded him about it. He didn't say anything."

"Tell me . . . did he ever mention the name Lodo to you at all?"

"Lodo?" She paused, then shook her head. "No, not Billings. But I've heard it somewhere. Who is he?"

"I don't know . . . yet. I'll find out, though."

This time she took my hand in both of hers. "Please be careful, Ryan."

"Sure, but why, kitten?"

"I might want to have lunch with a big hood again." She took her hand away with a smile, looked at her watch and reached for her pocketbook. "Time to leave. I'll make a quick visit first."

"Go ahead. I'll meet you up front."

Eddie Mack and Fats Sebull, a pair of guys I know, were talking to Pat and saw me coming. Fats said, "Pretty company you got."

"Great. She okay, Fats?"

"We had her checked. She's okay. One hell of a card player, though."

"That's what I hear."

Eddie Mack asked me, "How'd you meet her?"

"Checking on Billings."

He snorted. "Him. He won't be missed." He stopped, looked at me with a frown. "You knew him?"

"I wanted to kill him, buddy. I got beat out."

He glanced around him nervously and licked his lips. "Say, Ryan . . . you got any idea who tapped him?"

"An idea. A guy named Lodo. You ever hear of him?"

It was Pat's face that rang the bell. His eyes had a funny look and something had happened to the set of his mouth.

I said, "Pat?"

He motioned with his hand to keep it quiet. "Man, that's a trouble name."

"You know him?"

"I don't want to, kid, but a couple days ago two scared union representatives were in here and one made a phone call from the booths in back when I was in the office. He didn't know I was there, but I could hear him. When I bothered to listen, he was saying that there were some marked boys around and that Lodo had showed up. Apparently he had picked it up accidentally and he told the other guy he was clearing out."

"That was all?"

"Enough for me, friend. Any bumping I don't want done on the premises. I don't even want people around who know about them things. I've had all that crap I want."

"Don't get so shook, Patsy boy."

"Look, Ryan, if you're in this, then keep it someplace else."

I grinned and nodded.

Behind them Carmen was walking toward me and everybody in the place was watching her. She said, "Hello, Fats . . . Eddie. You know Ryan?"

Fats said, "We've met."

I nodded to them and walked out with her. We got into a cab. "Taking me to be verified by Fats and Eddie was smart. Are you satisfied?"

I looked at her and grinned. "Not satisfied at all, kitten."

Her smile came back fast. She reached over with her hand and pulled my head toward hers and suddenly there was a fire on my mouth that was alive and wet and a little shocking.

When she stopped it was too soon and she said, "I never kissed a hood before, either." She touched my mouth with a finger. "Satisfied now?"

"No," I said, and I grinned.

"You're cool, big boy, real big and ugly and cool, man."

"That's not VP talk, sugar."

"I thought maybe you'd understand it better," she mocked.

"Talk punk language then," I said.

For a moment she was serious. "You're no punk. I've known punks before."

"Oh?"

"I could get to like you, big man. But never a punk."

The cab had stopped. I said, "We're here."

"Will I see you again?" Her eyes wanted me to say yes.

"If you say please."

She smiled and touched my mouth with her finger again. "Please."

"I'll call you."

"I'll be waiting. Will you be long?"

"When I find a guy named Lodo."

"Be careful."

"Sure."

She got out and walked away. Her legs were long and her hips wide and with each stride her thighs would play against the fabric of her dress and it was almost as if she had nothing on at all.

I had the cab take me back to DiNuccio's. Art wasn't there, but Joe told me he had called my place a couple times without any luck, then went out.

I grabbed a quick beer, waved to Joe and went out to the corner hoping to catch a crosstown cab.

That was when I knew I had picked up a tail.

He was a small guy in a plastic raincoat with a folded paper sticking up out of the pocket. He hadn't been on the ball and when he first spotted me, his involuntary start tagged him. To make sure, I hesitated on the corner, then turned and walked west. He stayed with me, checking over his shoulder for a cab.

When one came, he caught it, rode to the corner and stopped. I knew he was waiting for me to get the next one and when I passed him he'd hang on. It would've been fun if I had more time. Instead, I turned, went back to the corner and picked up a hack just letting out a passenger. The Brooks Brothers Boys were determined to get their progress report the hard way.

The drizzle turned into a hard rain before I got to the apartment. The street was empty and even Pete-the-Dog was gone to hawk his papers around the bars. I paid off the driver, got my key out and ran for the entrance. I went inside, flipped the light on and knew I had it.

The two sitting there had their rods out smashing slugs over my head and swearing at the dive I had made to one side which put one guy in the way of the other. I rolled once behind a chair, kicked it at them and saw the top rip off it from a slug, then I had my own gun out and cocked and the chubby little guy in front caught a fat .45 dead in the chest. The other one ran for the door and I got him through both knees and he lay there screaming his lungs out until I cracked him across the mouth with the muzzle of the automatic.

He kept saying over and over again. *"Marone, marone!"*

Behind me the other one coughed once, then was still.

I said, "It doesn't really hurt yet. Give it a couple hours."

He pulled his hands away from his knees, looked at the blood and tried to reach for the rod he had dropped. I kicked it out of the way. His eyes were terrible things trying to kill me all by themselves.

32

I raised the .45 and pointed it at his gut. "Who sent you, bud?"

"*Go . . .*"

"Watch it. I'm no sweet law-abiding citizen. Knocking you off wouldn't be a bit hard. I even got a license for my rod. Figure it out quick, buddy, because you haven't got much time left at all."

He looked at his hands again and gagged, then fell over on his side. "I need a doctor . . ."

"You'll need an undertaker more."

"Look . . ."

"Talk." My hand started to go white around the butt.

"Ryan . . . it was orders . . . it was . . ." Somehow he knew it was coming. He threw one wild look around before the blast from the doorway caught him. I got out of the line before it could happen to me, then the lights went out and the door slammed shut.

I might have made it at that, but the dead guy in the doorway tripped me and I went down. When I threw the main fuse lever back in place and got outside, there was nobody on the street at all.

The shadows across the street moved a little bit and I went over. Razztazz, the crippled guy, was hunkered back in his basement doorway his shoulders twitching. I said, "You see him, Razz?"

"Went to the corner, Ryan. Soon's you went in a car was standing by. Picked him up."

"You make any of them?"

"One I knew."

"Who?"

"Lardbucket Pearson, the fat guy."

"How'd you know him? You can't see faces from across here now."

"Not by that. It was his big butt and the way he walked. Cop shot him in the behind once. He ain't never walked right since."

"I don't know him, Razz."

"Part of the Jersey crowd where I come from. Always was in the rackets around the docks." He wiped his hand across his face. "They . . . still there?"

"Yeah. Dead."

"Couldn't hear anything from here at all. The fuzz coming along?"

"Let me work it out. Keep it quiet."

"You know me, Ryan."

I stuck a folded bill into his pocket and slapped his shoulder. He grinned and nodded and I went back into the rain.

Neither one of the punks had anything on them at all. No wallets, no labels, no papers of any kind. In their own way they were farsighted pros—but they'd finally walked into the inevitable occupational hazard.

I reloaded the .45, threw a handful of shells in my pocket and looked at them. Things were beginning to look up. It takes a while, but the pattern gets set and starts to look like something. When I had the idea rounded out, I flicked off the light and went out to the vestibule. The rain had made an effective muffler for the sound. There were no curious faces in the windows . . . no movement anywhere, and no sounds of sirens hanging in the air.

At the corner I hung back in the folds of darkness that draped the building there. Traffic was light, nothing more than a few occupied cabs moving with the lights. Nobody was on the sidewalks.

For five minutes I stayed there, watching, then across the street somebody hacked and vomited then painfully unfolded from being a doorway bundle to one of the bums you see around occasionally. He edged toward Second Ave., leaning against the building, then got on his own and wobbled off the curb and started across the street.

Down the block a car pulled away from the curb, flicked on its lights so the beams spotlighted the guy. Just as quickly it cut back to the curb and doused them.

They were waiting for me. Behind me on First would be others.

I was on a kill list now. Someplace along the line I had gotten big enough and important enough to be in somebody's way. Someplace I did something, or I saw something, or I thought something. Someplace I had reached a conclusion that made me ready for the big bed.

Mamie Huggins never bothered to lock her basement entrance. I took a chance on not being seen and went back and down through her basement. There was one low fence to cross and I came out the alley between Benny's grocery and the building they were tearing down.

When the block was empty, I crossed again and used the alley where Jamie Tohey kept his laundry pushcarts. I went all the way through, turned west when I reached the street and went back to Second again. Up near my own corner the car still waited. I grinned at it and walked south to Hymie's drug store.

After five tries I reached Art through his office and told him what had happened. Tension was evident in his voice when he asked me what I wanted.

I said, "Get me what you can on a character named Lardbucket Pearson. He'll probably have Jersey connections."

"Sure. What about the stiffs in your apartment? You can't let 'em lie there and it's damn sure nobody's going to just stumble over them."

"Why don't you do it, Art?"

"Do what?"

"Make a call at my place and find them. Any one of the sheets would buy a news beat with photos for the bit."

"You crazy? Listen . . ."

"You listen. Do it. Otherwise I'll call a guy with the wire services. Give me twenty-four hours to think, then do it."

He breathed hard into the receiver before he answered me. "Okay, friend, but it's blood money. You'll have the cops screaming for your hair."

"That'll make it unanimous."

"Where can I get in touch with you?"

"Use the Naples Cafe on Second Street. They'll take any messages."

I hung up, reached for the phone book and flipped through it until I found the only Carmen Smith and dialed the number. I let it ring a good while before I hung up feeling a little sour.

The other number was Jake McGaffney. He wasn't doing anything and said to come on up. It took me 20 minutes and my feet got soaking wet.

He looked at my face and said, "Wha' hoppen, boy?"

I told him. He made himself a drink and opened me a beer.

"This hitting my business, Ryan?"

"I don't think so. If that tap on Gonzales didn't do it, then you're clear enough."

"You're trying to make a point someplace."

"Where was Gonzales collecting for you?"

"Oh, light spots, mostly. He had a string of bars . . . let's say about twenty, and a few other places in his own neighborhood."

"Did he work around the docks?"

"Gonzales? Hell, no. I'm not doing any field work in that area. That's uptown stuff."

"That's what I thought. How much did he usually have on hand?"

Jake shrugged and made a face. "He'd pay off two-three hundred every day, bring back five. Small time, but with plenty small guys working, we stay in business, y'know?"

"Was he square?"

"A dream to have working. Never clipped a dime, and that I know." He sipped at his drink. "What's all this traffic with Gonzales, Ryan?"

"He had a dream too . . . of him and his broad taking a trip around the world, really living it up."

"*Him*? On what? He never had anything."

"He had ten grand."

"Hell, you can't even do Miami right on ten . . ." He stopped, put his drink down and stared at me. "Where'd he get ten grand?"

"I think from a guy named Billings."

"I don't get it."

"Don't worry about it. Neither do I. One other thing. Does the name Lodo mean anything to you?"

Jake's memory for names was too good for him to think long. He shook his head and there was nothing more to say.

The cabs were slower now. I saw one stopped for the light, ran across the street and climbed in. The address I gave was Lucinda Gonzales' and when I got out the street was quiet, like a sick dog.

There was a light on under Lucinda's door and when I knocked a chair scraped back.

She smiled vacantly and I could smell the whiskey on her. I pushed the door shut behind me and said, "Lucinda?"

"You still have your money?"

She sat down heavily and brushed her hair back. "Si . . . but it is no good now without Juan."

"Lucinda . . . who has been here to see you?"

"To see me? Oh . . . the neighbors. They come. From uptown my cousin, he comes."

"Any of Juan's friends?"

"They are peegs, señor."

"Do you know who they are?"

"Sure." She swayed and tried to get up. "They are off the boat." She leaned hard against the table, balancing herself. "One is 'Fredo. Other is Spanish Tom. They are peegs, señor. They theenk I am listening to them and they hit me. Juan, he does not even care."

I circled the table and held on to her. "What boat, Lucinda?"

She shrugged and reached for the bottle. Her unsteady hand knocked it over and she started to cry. I eased her back into the chair and let her pass out with her head pressed into her forearms.

When I reached Times Square, I stopped, deciding which hotel to use. I settled on the Chessy on 49th and took off that way. Before I reached the end of the first block, I knew I had somebody behind me.

He came up fast, passed me and said, "Ryan," without turning his head. He crossed against the lights, hesitated, then jaywalked all the way to the east side of the street.

When nobody could have made any connection I crossed over myself, went down to 47th and turned the corner leisurely. Then I stopped and flattened against the wall.

Nothing. I gave it another two minutes before I went to where Diego Flores was waiting for me in the shadows.

36

He was more scared than nervous and his beady little eyes kept poking into the night on either side of him. Diego ran numbers for Sid Solomon on the Madison Avenue run and usually he was a pretty calm guy.

I said, "Hi, Dago. What's the fuss?"

He tapped my chest with a forefinger. "Baby . . . you got rocks in your head. Big fat rocks. What you doin' in town?"

"Why leave, kid?"

"Ain't you heard it yet? Ryan baby, what happened to all those big ears you had?"

"I'm listening now."

"Baby . . . whoever throws you down makes five grand. The world's out on you."

"Who says, Dago?"

"None of our bunch, Baby. This one's comin' in the hard way. It's all over town. First thing, the nose candy kids'll be tryin' for the tap. You got marked poison somehow and unless you blow out you're dead."

"Where's it come from?"

"Picked it up at Bimmy's. You know Stan Etching?" I nodded and he went on. "Him and that nutty brother of his was talkin' about it. Since they knocked off Fletcher over in Canarsie they're big stuff. Anyway, they're working now and you're their job. Everybody's gonna be trying for you, baby."

"Why not you, Dago?"

"Ah, baby, come off it. You favored me up plenty times when I had troubles."

"How hot is it?"

"You better not go anyplace you're known. They even got the hotels spotted. You're a big one."

"Okay, kid, thanks. Shove off before you get tied in to me."

He glanced around again and licked his lips. "Baby . . . be careful, will ya? I can smell this stink. It's from way up, ya know? Ya can tell, somethin's burning in this town."

"Yeah."

When he walked off, I gave him five minutes and cruised past the Chessy. I spotted Manny Golden in the foyer and his partner Willis Holmes across the street talking to a cab driver outside the Ployden House. Both were ex-cops busted out in the graft scandal in '49. Now they were hoods. Not cheap ones, either. They still held a few things over important precinct heads and could move around pretty good when they wanted to.

Just to be sure I made a few of the other pads off Broadway and when I saw Mario Sen, I knew just how hot I was. Mario's specialty was big kills and he didn't operate for under 10 grand per. That is, outside his regular job.

Mario was a tap man for the Mafia.

Mario didn't seem to have any place to go specially so I helped
him out. I stuck my gun in his back and steered him to the men's
room in the back of the lobby.

He was real embarrassed.

I let him turn around and have a good look at me and said,
"You got yourself a big one this time, buddy." Then I smashed
him across the face with the rod and when he went down choking
noisily, I whipped the gun across his skull until he stopped.

He was going to be a sick hood. Sicker when his boss found out.

The envelope held an even grand in fifties. It fitted my pocket
nicely. There was nothing new about the rest of the contents.
They were photos of me. Police photos. Something Golden or
Holmes dug up, probably. I flushed them down the toilet, frisked
Mario and lifted another $400 from his poke and added it to my
pile.

It was turning out to be a good evening.

I grabbed a cab outside, went to 23rd St., walked crosstown
two blocks and took another one back. The third one let me out
on the corner of Carmen Smith's block.

I told the officious little man at the desk I wished to see Miss
Smith and that it was important enough that he should call and
waken her. He didn't believe me at first, then I smiled and he
believed me.

Carmen answered the house phone, asked to speak to me and
when I said hello, told me to come right up. The little man was
still nervous so I put her on and let her tell him it was okay. He
clacked his teeth and escorted me to the elevator and showed me
which button to push. I said thanks and pushed it.

She was waiting in the tiny foyer that separated her apartment
from the elevator. She said, "Well, hello! And if you don't mind
the obvious, what brings you here?"

I grinned at her. "I need a place to sleep."

"Oh," she said, and opened the door wide. "Come on in."

She had on a tailored, double-breasted housecoat that fitted
without a fold or a crease and when she walked, the static of her
body against the cloth made it cling so that you knew she slept
cool and naked and inviting.

Like beautiful girls should be, she was unruffled from sleep,
still bearing the flush of lipstick. She walked ahead of me into
the living room and she was tall even without shoes. When she
turned on the light on the end table, there was a momentary
silhouette that made me stop and look around quickly, merely
sensing the expensive appointments of the place rather than
appreciating them.

Carmen looked at me quizzically a moment. Then she *knew*.
She smiled gently and waved me to a chair. She brought a drink
without a word, handed it to me and sat down.

38

Then, very deliberately, she grinned and crossed her legs.
I could have smacked her in the mouth.

She said, "Okay, hood, what do you want from me?" Then her grin turned into a small laugh that made the mood easier.

"Kid, you can get in real trouble doing that."

"You mean the leg action."

"Don't get smart."

She made a kiss with her mouth and blew it across the room. "Now really, why did you come up?"

"I'm in a bind."

The smile softened, then worked into a frown. "Police?"

"A little worse, sugar. The sign's on me."

She didn't need any explanation. She took a few seconds letting it sink in and there was something tight about the way she held herself. "Bad?"

"Real bad. They called out the troops."

Her eyes crinkled thoughtfully. She got up, took my glass and refilled it. When she handed it to me, she said, "Will it help to tell me?"

"No, but I will." And I told her.

She sat wordlessly a moment, then: "What can I do, Ryan?"

"Pack me in for the night, kitten, I don't like to be shot when I'm sleeping, and all my usual pads are off limits now."

"That's all?" She stood up and studied me with the edge of her forefinger between her teeth.

I stood up too and took her hand away. "No, there's more, but I wouldn't inflict it on you, sugar."

She was there in my arms without seeming to move. Suddenly she was just there, pressing tightly against me and she was warm and woman and I could feel the life inside her. Her finger touched my mouth, then her own. "Why, Ryan?"

Softly, I said, "For a hood I got certain sensitivities."

She reached up and kissed me lightly. She smiled, did it again and took my arm under hers. She showed me the guest room and opened the door.

Once more she came back into my arms. "I have certain sensitivities too. I wish you would inflict them on me."

"Later."

Her mouth was warm and very wet. "All right, later." Lightly, she touched my lips with her tongue, deliberately tantalizing.

Her grin got impish and she did something with her hands. Then she shrugged and handed me the housecoat, stepped back and smiled again. She walked away from me into the light, turned into her room and was gone.

When I began to breathe again, I tossed the housecoat on a chair, took a real cold shower and went to bed. Before I could sleep my mind dwelt on the litheness of her, the swaying stride, the lush, yet muscular curves that seemed to melt into each other and dance in the subdued, shadowy tones of dark and light. Brunette, I thought, a luscious, chestnut-hued brunette.

The radio alarm beside the bed went off softly. Awakening, I knew where I was at once, knowing, too, that I had never set the alarm. But the door was partly open and the housecoat gone, so I knew who had. The note on the clock was brief. It said, *Call me, hood.* And the P.S. was just as brief. She had written, *You look pretty.* There were no covers on the bed and now we were even for the housecoat.

Coffee was ready in the electric perc and there were some Danish in a basket. While I grabbed a bite, I called the Naples Cafe, got a number for me to call Art and dialed it.

In the background there were morning noises of people eating, and strange, loud languages. There was juke music and somebody yelling and Art was drunk. He was all-night drunk, but purpose-drunk and there's a difference. He felt his way through his words, mouthing each one. "Ryan . . . I got what you wanted."

"Good. Let's have it."

"You see the papers?"

"Not yet."

"Those punks . . . you hit . . . your place?"

"Yeah?"

"Cullen and . . . and Stanovich. From Elizabeth, Jersey, y'know? Muscle boys . . . docks. This here . . . Lardbucket Pearson . . . him . . . I mean, he and Turner Scado car piled into . . . big ditch outside Hoboken. They got killed. Looks like your boys . . . muff it, they get it."

The picture was clear enough. It even made the deal bigger than ever. When somebody can afford to knock off help who flubbed, it was big time, real big-time.

I said, "What's their connections, Art?"

He fumbled against the phone for a second. "Topside Big. It reaches, Ryan. Goes far . . . to . . . to Europe."

"What names, kid?"

I could hear ice clink in a glass, then he paused to swallow. He finally said, "Those Jersey Joes . . . Mafia musclemen. Used to be part of . . . Lucky's crew. You know what that means?"

"It's making sense. What else?"

He laughed sourly. "I'm gonna . . . beat you . . . on this one, Irish. I have a friend in Rome. Good friend. In their organization over there. For . . . American cash . . . he's tipping me to your mysterious buddy."

"What buddy?"

"Lodo," he chuckled. "Lodo . . . pretty big stuff. Lodo's . . . code name for Mafia's East coast enforcer. Big killer. Little while I'll know who."

I said, "Okay. Go home and stay there. You hear?"

"I'll go slow." He paused a moment, coughed and said, "You're lucky, Irish."

"How?"

"You're going to get to die real . . . soon."

I hopped a cab to 34th St., picked up an envelope at General Delivery in the Post Office and opened it on the street.

The laddies were real efficient. Usually it took a month to get a gun permit. This one came through quick. I tucked it in my pocket and looked at the other slip of paper. There were seven digits there, and the first two had to be exchange letters. I found a pay phone and dialed.

A male voice said, "Yes?"

I said, "Big Man?"

He said, "That you, Ryan?"

"Me. And don't trace this."

His voice sounded strained. "What do you need, Irish?"

"Two guys. They work a ship that was in around the week a certain Juan Gonzales was killed. All I know is the alias. One's Spanish Tom, the other 'Fredo . . . probably Alfredo. You big enough to handle it?"

"We're big enough."

I left the booth, walked to the corner and had two minutes before the unmarked cruiser drew up and the guys hopped out. Another one blocked off the street at the other end and a fast, systematic search started. I laughed at the slobs and walked away. Big Man was playing both ends from the middle.

I gave him an hour. It was plenty of time. They had men and equipment and millions and could do nearly any damn thing they wanted when they wanted.

I called and said, "Big Man?"

He said, "Both men are on the *Gastry*. It's in port now. Spanish Tom is Tomas Escalante. The other one is Alfredo Lias. Both from Lisbon. They've been on the same ship since '46. Both have had numerous drunk arrests in various ports but nothing more serious. The line vouches for their honesty."

"Thanks. You haven't bothered to look for them, have you?"

He caught the sarcasm. "They're in port, Ryan. We've been looking but so far we haven't found them."

I laughed. "What would you ask them if you did?"

"We'd think of something."

"Good for you," I said. "There's just one more thing I never bothered asking. You guys don't operate without certain facts or at the most without ideas."

"So?"

"What did you suspect Billings of having for sale?"

Quietly, he said, "A month ago two skin divers were killed going down on the wreck of the *Andrea Doria*."

"I read about it."

"There were three on the expedition. The last one hasn't shown."

"Go on."

"It should be obvious. Highly classified material went down in that wreck and if found by the wrong parties could jeopardize the safety of the whole country. Possibly the whole world."

After a moment he said, "That enough?"

I said, "That's enough," and hung up.

Nobody was outside and I walked away from the phone thinking about it. There were just too many possibilities now. Some of them had to go. I walked slowly and let things dribble through my mind. A pattern began to come out of it.

Further down the street I stepped into another phone booth, rang the apartment to see if Art was there. I let it ring a dozen times then decided he was either asleep or passed out, then gave up.

I picked up a paper from a newsstand. They had given me pretty good coverage. Pictures and all.

Police opinion seemed to be that it was a gang killing of some kind, that I had been poaching in foreign fields. There was speculation that I had been taken for an old-fashioned ride. So far their leads were lousy.

So was their liaison. The big agency upstairs that had conned me into this rumble wasn't talking either.

Natural coloration is the animal's best protection. In the slop chutes that were the playgrounds for the dock crowd I fitted smooth and easy. They could smell money on you, they knew you were brand new to the neighborhood, but all the time they knew the other thing they saw in your face. You just weren't takable.

A couple I knew, tough apples who'd work any kind of a touch for pocket money. They passed me over with a nod and gave me room at the bar.

If the word was out all the way, it hadn't reached here yet. But maybe they were figuring it the usual way . . . a hood hates to leave his own back yard. Every step away from his own hole and he becomes more vulnerable. His own distorted sense of security that led him into a hole in the first place makes him stay close to it even when he's dying.

There could be another reason too. New York was a big town. The word can only travel just so fast . . . and it wasn't good to think about it. Any time now the posters could go up and in this section hired guns were handy to get to.

The pair I spoke to on the *Gastry* didn't have much to say about Escalante or Lias. As far as they knew, all they did in port was visit around the Spanish-speaking sections and get gassed up. Neither had steady women or much to do with the rest of the crew.

Neither one of them was very smart. Both were dull, plodding types who were at the peak of their earning capacity in the grimy hold of the freighter.

It just didn't figure right. They weren't 10-grand types. They weren't international types. They weren't the type anybody should get excited about or interested in for any damn reason whatsoever. Their being around at all had all the earmarks of a crazy, distracting coincidence like a fly in the soup but until I found them I couldn't be sure.

A long time ago I learned how to get answers without ever having to ask the questions. But it took time. It took me from 57th Street down to the Battery and halfway back and by then it was night again with the same damn rain thick with dirt and soot that steamed up from the pavement and got inside your clothes.

But I found Spanish Tom. He was in the middle of a crowd of dock workers and the center of attraction, sitting on the pavement with his back against the overhead highway support and if you didn't see the hole in him right away you'd think he was sleeping.

The uniformed cop taking notes squatted and held his coat open with the tip of his pencil and for a moment everybody quieted down and craned to see the business better. It was quite a tap, a real professional job, one hard knife jab under the ribs and up into the heart and that was the end.

I worked my way through to the front and stood there trying to figure the angle on it. I kind of started a trend and a few more wanted in close and when the cop stood up he yelled for everybody to get the hell away. He scared the half-drunk sailor beside me and he nudged the body and Spanish Tom flopped sideways on the pavement and one leg kicked out like he was still alive.

The cop yelled again and shoved the nearest ones away. He turned to me, but by then I had already backed off and the pasteboard ticket that had come out of Spanish Tom's pocket was under my foot. I scraped it back, retrieved it, and squeezed back through the crowd.

In the one second I saw it I had thought it was a pawn slip, but when I got back under the light I could have spit. It was an ADMIT TWO in Spanish to some shindig up in the quarter. I

43

crumbled it in my fist and threw it back in the gutter and mouthed a curse at it.

Then I thought about it again and picked it up. If Alfredo Lias had one of these too it could be the place he'd be at. The date was tomorrow; the place a bloody-up with an olê olê band. The clientele was the kind you saw in the tabloids leaning up against a wall while the fuzz frisked them.

But that was tomorrow. I had *now* to think about. Until tomorrow I had to stay out of sight of everybody and it wasn't going to be easy. I flagged a cab down, gave an address a block away from Art's and got out on an empty corner.

Halfway down I found the Wheeler Apartments and touched Art's bell. The vestibule door was open so before he could answer I went ahead up. I knocked at his door and waited, knocked again and listened for him stirring around.

There wasn't a sound from inside.

I tried the door and the knob turned under my hand. I pushed it open, stepped inside, shut it behind me and waited there in the semi-gloom of the room. It was too still, much too still. I pulled the .45 out already cocked and held it ready, then flicked on the light.

Nothing.

It wasn't much of a place. Something a bachelor would have. One main room with the kitchen separated from it by a bar, an open door leading to the bath and another door, cracked a little, going to the bedroom.

I walked over to that one, pushed it open the rest of the way and reached for the light switch inside the frame.

And then I found Art.

The spare pillow beside him showed powder burns and one corner had been ripped off from the bullet blast the pillow had muffled. It had caught him in the temple and without ever realizing it Art had reached the goal he had striven for.

All I could say was one word. There was nothing else. I was being hung higher all the time. Nobody knew I told Art to make a feature yarn out of the kills at my place and now the fuzz would lay this tap at my door and label it a revenge kill. Whoever coined the word *shafted* had me in mind.

There was a whiskey, cordite and burnt feathers smell still in the air, a smell that could hang for hours. I felt Art's face, knew by the heat of it that death came only a short time ago. I went back to the door to see if it had been forced, but there were no marks around the lock. Art had made it easy for the killer. He had come home drunk, opened up and shut the door. The lock was a type you had to hand turn from the inside to latch and he had done what a thousand other drunks did before him. He forgot about it. He flopped in bed and that was it.

I went through his pockets carefully, tried his jacket thrown over a chair, then the clothes in the closet. There was something not quite orderly enough about the clothes in his dresser and I knew that all this had been done earlier by an expert and if there had been anything important, it was gone now.

I wiped the spots I had touched with my handkerchief and backed out of the apartment. I went upstairs and over the roof to a building near the corner and came out there in case anybody was waiting for me outside Art's place. Two blocks further down I found a cab and gave him Carmen's number.

The important little man remembered me from before, but even then he double-checked. He told me reluctantly that Miss Smith would see me, then huffed away, so supreme in his own importance that he never recognized me even with the paper on his desk open to my picture.

I went upstairs to where she was waiting and grinned at the worry that showed around her eyes. Then suddenly she was tight inside my arms and her mouth was a hungry thing tasting me almost painfully, her body taut with life that has been confined too long and for the first time senses a release.

Tears made glistening streaks down her cheeks and when she took her mouth from mine she kept it open, sobbing against my neck.

I said, "Easy, baby," and held her away to look at her, but only for a second because she grabbed me again and hung on fiercely.

Very softly she repeated over and over, "You crazy hood. You crazy hood, you!"

I wiped off the tears, kissed her lightly, then took her arm and went inside. There was still a sob in her breathing and she wasn't ready to talk to me yet. I said, "I'm not used to such pleasant receptions."

She forced a smile, then it became real. "You crazy Irishman. Every paper, every TV newscaster, every radio broadcast has you in it. Ryan . . . you haven't got a chance . . . you haven't . . . I don't know how to put it . . ."

"It's bad, huh?"

"Why, Ryan? Why does it have to be you?"

"Why all the concern, sugar?"

She said nothing for a moment. Her eyes frowned and she took her hand from mine and folded them in her lap. "I'm not the type who should do something like this. I know better. I've been familiar with . . . wrong situations a whole lifetime. It's never happened before. Now, for the first time I know what it's like, having to . . . care for somebody who feels nothing, well, very special about you. It's happened to others. I never thought it could possibly happen to me." She looked up, smiled and added lightly, "And with a hood too. I've never been in love with a hood before."

"You're crazy."

"I know," she said.

"You're class, baby. With me a fling could be fun. Some excitement, like playing cards, maybe. But sugar . . . like I'm not the kind of slob kids like you fall in love with. You're class."

"Irish . . . you've never had trouble getting a woman . . . ever. Have you?"

I squinted and shook my head. "Tomatoes, though."

"So let me be a tomato. Or should I ask please?"

"You're talking crazy, girl."

"I have nothing else, Irish. I never had."

"Hell, I could be cut down any time. You know what that means? You get connected with me and you're done, kid. Done. Maybe it's like you said . . . you've never been in love with a hood before, but it's like the excitement of drawing three cards from the dealer and finding yourself with a royal flush. It's great if the stakes are high, but when the other hands are twos and threes and go out on a small pot the big excitement is all wasted. It only seemed big. It wasn't worth anything. Damn it, you're crazy!"

I was tight on talk and that scar on my back began to draw up again. I had to tell her. She knew what the score was!

Carmen's eyes were clear now. While I was talking she had made up her mind. She said, "Will you let me be a crazy tomato, Irish?"

"Kitten . . ."

"You don't have to love me back at all," she said.

I tried hard to keep it inside. I didn't want to let it out, but it wasn't the kind of thing you can squash into pieces and forget. "That's the bad part, kid," I told her. "You see . . . I do."

She was there in my arms again, softly at first and hungry-mouthed again. Her fingers were velvet cat claws, kneading me gently, searching and finding. When I touched her, things seemed to melt away until there was only the warmth of flesh and a giddy sensation of being overpowered by a runaway emotion. As I lay there, time ceased to exist and as she came down on top of me she murmured little things only the mind heard and it was different. So very different.

Morning was a soft light that bathed us both, and we got up smiling, yet saying nothing. Words were no good any more. I watched her shower and dress. All the naked, all the clothed beauty of her belonged to me and nobody could take it away.

Then the luxury of sleep-drugged morning was over and I knew how stupid it was and the vomit sour taste of cold hate for all the things that had happened to me was in my mouth.

I dressed quickly and followed her into the kitchen. She had coffee ready and handed me a cup, knowing by my face that something was wrong. She didn't ask. She waited until I was ready. I said, "I had a friend who was killed last night. I know how, I know why and I know who, but I don't know what the killer's face is like."

"Can I help somehow?"

"You can but I won't ask you. The gamble is too big."

"You forgot, Irish?"

"What?"

"I *am* a gambler."

"That kill is going to be laid at my feet and there isn't a chance in the world for me to cut out."

"The police . . ."

"Can be stalled a while. They can be stymied, but only for a while. When they concentrate all the resources of their system, they can do anything."

"You think they will?"

"They have to, baby. Now it's a newshawk who's dead and the papers will hammer the brass silly. They have to shake that heat and the only way is to find me."

"But first we gamble."

I looked at her hard. She wasn't kidding. I said, "Okay, baby, it'll be you and me. We'll give it a try. Maybe we can make the good parts come out."

"What will we do?"

"Tonight's Saturday night, kid. We're going dancing." A puzzled frown creased her forehead. "You'll need a costume for the act, sugar. Where we'll be you'll want the west side trollop look. Think you can make it?"

She nodded, the frown deepening.

"A missing link was killed last night," I continued. "He had a dance ticket in his pocket. Chances are his partner had one too. On top of which, if he knows his buddy's dead, he'll want to be with a crowd. It's easy to die alone."

"This one . . . he can clear you?"

I grinned at that one. "Not him. But this bird can supply a lot of answers."

"Then what can I do?"

"First you can go out and buy some clothes. Cheap and flashy. Get perfume and accessories to match and if you can get the stuff secondhand, do that. Guys alone at those jumps can't move around the way a couple can and locating this guy will be easier with two of us asking questions."

I took her shoulders and looked into her eyes. "Still want to try it?"

She grinned impishly, made like she was going to give me a tiny kiss, then stuck her tongue in my mouth. Before my hands could tighten on her she pulled away and went to the door.

"You'll stay here?"

"I don't know."

She opened her purse, took out a key and tossed it to me. "If you come in the back way you can by-pass the clerk." She blew a kiss and was gone.

I got up, yanked my coat on and shoved the .45 under my belt. I went out the back way and headed for the old brownstone. The sun died before I reached Sixth and the air had a cold, clammy touch to it. I stopped at a candy store and had a Coke, then another, trying to think the pieces together.

A pattern was there, all right. Crude and irregular, but it had a purpose.

Outside it began to rain again.

A beat cop sauntered by and looked in, but I was in the shadows and my face didn't mean a thing to him. When he was gone, I picked up my change and walked out, my collar up around my neck, the hatbrim screening my face.

I was almost at Lexington when they had me. It worked real easy, the faint nudge of a gun barrel in a hand with a paper around it and that was all there was to it.

I looked around and Stan Etching was smiling at me, the scar on his chin pulling his mouth out of shape. He said, "They told me you were a tough guy, Ryan." He stepped around in front of me, lifted out the gun and dropped it in his raincoat pocket.

His smile was nervous and I knew what he was thinking. It was almost too easy. I said, "Now what?"

"You'll see. My brother Stash saw me grab you, feller. He'll be here with the car in a minute. Maybe you'd like it better to run or something."

I grinned and his eyes got nervous along with his mouth. "I'll wait," I said.

The car was a three-year-old Caddie sedan with Jersey plates. It pulled up noiselessly and Stan opened the back door. I got in and he sat on my right, his gun pointed at my belly.

When we pulled away from the curb Stash turned the radio up and said, "How'd he take it?"

"Like pie. How else?" He poked me with the gun and grinned. "You're a chump, Ryan. You shoulda hid out. Me, I knew you'd

ome back though. Six of us had your dump staked out, but I
ven knew which way you'd come."

"This is the old Chicago touch you're giving it," I said. "One
way ride and all that crap."

He laughed. "Sure. Glad you don't feel bad about it. Hey
Stash, this guy's all right." The gun bumped me again. "You
know, Ryan, I'm gonna burn you out quick. No fooling around.
You give me no trouble. I give you no trouble."

I told him thanks and leaned back in the seat and watched
Stash approach the Lincoln Tunnel. Traffic was heavy.

Stan looked across at me and grinned again, turning a little to
point the rod square at me. I took a deep breath of disgust,
leaned back further into the cushions and completely relaxed.

Then I moved my hand before he could pull the trigger,
slammed back the slide on the automatic so it couldn't fire,
twisted it so his finger broke and while he was still screaming
with surprise and pain, shoved the muzzle against his gut and
pulled the trigger.

Up front Stash let out a crazy startled yell and tried to look
back, but there wasn't a thing he could do, not a damn, stinking
thing. I got my .45 back from Stan, cocked it and let Stan feel
the big "O" of the mouth of it against his neck. His head jerked
like a spastic's and he kept making funny little noises.

I said, "When we get out, I'll tell you where to go. Don't do
anything silly."

He didn't. He stayed calmly hysterical and when we reached
the scrap iron works in Secaucus, we stopped and I let him get
in the back. The shock was wearing off and Stan's face was white
with pain and fear. He kept asking for a doctor, but I shook my
head.

Stash said, "What'cha gonna do?"

"It depends on you. I want to know about the word. Who put
it out?"

Stash looked hopelessly at his brother. Stan said, ". . . doctor."

"Not yet. Maybe when you talk a little."

It began to dawn on Stan gradually. I wasn't kidding. He
shook his head feebly. "I told ya. Nothin'. You know . . . how
them things are."

I raised the gun again and watched his eyes. He couldn't even
speak, but he was telling it straight. I said, "Who else is around
my place and where?"

"Golden . . . and Holmes. They're on the south end. Lou
Steckler, he's . . . across in . . . in the gimp's house."

My hand got tight on the gun. "What'd they do to Razztazz?"

"Geeze . . . I dunno . . . I . . ."

"Who else? Dammit, talk fast!"

"Mario . . . he's in your dump."

"No fuzz?"

"Nobody. They . . . they got pulled off. Hymie the Goose he's covering trains and all with his bunch. Babcock and . . . the Greek . . . they . . . Jersey. They . . ."

He fainted then. I gave him five minutes and let him come around. He started to retch and vomited all down his chest. Stash was still hysterical and shook all over.

I said, "What else, Stan?"

He shook his head.

There wasn't any more and I knew it. I told Stash to get out of the car and walk around the side. I had him pull his brother out and they stood there like animals watching me. I said, "Whenever and wherever I see you again, you catch one between the antlers, buddies. I don't think I'll have to worry about it because somebody else will get to you first like with them Elizabeth hoods. Now beat it."

Stan's eyes went wide. "Jeez . . . ain't you even gonna call a doc? Ain't you . . ."

"They were right when they said I was a tough guy."

"Ryan . . . Ryan . . ."

I started the car up. "Drop dead," I told him.

I took the car back through the tunnel and parked it on a cross street. When I wiped the wheel, door handles and sills off I climbed out and left it there. I found a phone, dialed the number I wanted and said, "Big Man?"

"Ryan . . ."

"Okay, Big Man, just listen for once. Where can we meet?"

"It's no good."

"Brother, I'm going to blow the whistle if you don't square off."

He paused. He didn't muffle the phone to talk to anyone or anything. He just sat there a minute, then: "We'll see you."

"Just you, friend."

"Where?"

"The Naples Cafe. It's on . . ."

"I know."

"Okay, then. Have a squad standing by a phone, but first you come alone. Quick."

He hung up without answering. I hopped a cab to the Naples and stood across the street. In 10 minutes another cab came along and the big man got out. He walked inside and when I was fairly certain nobody else was around, I crossed over and went inside. He was sitting there at a table with a cup of coffee in front of him, waiting.

I said, "It's not so snotty like the first time, is it?"

His face was hard. "Let's hear it, Ryan."

For some reason I wasn't edgy any more. I put my face in my hands and rubbed hard, then leaned on the table and stared at him. "Art Shay was killed," I said.

He nodded again. "We know. The police think you did it."

"Who found him?"

"Young kid upstairs who used his typewriter. Trying to be a free-lance writer. He's clean."

"So am I. No alibi. No proof. I'm just saying."

He tried one on me for size. "Spanish Tom showed up."

"Yeah, dead."

"You get around. We squelched the story."

"I was there right after it happened."

His eyes slitted a little bit. "What did you know about him?"

"Nothing, but I'll damn soon find out."

"How?"

"I'm pretty sure I know where his partner will be tonight."

"You want to tell me?"

"Not me, Big Man. I'm going all the way on this party."

"All right, Ryan, what did you want to call this . . . this meeting for?"

I sat back and sucked in my breath. "I want some answers. I want them straight and to the point. I have a funny feeling that I've touched something someplace and I'm close to what I want. I never did like any part of this business, but I'm in it all the way and if I want to stay alive and you want to get your answers, check me off with the truth."

He made a short gesture with his hand. "Go ahead."

"Was I suckered into this thing with big talk or because I was suspect?"

For a moment he looked at my face, then made his decision. "A little of both. You were suspect because you were brought into it by Billings. We had to grasp at straws no matter how small."

"Why?"

"You know why. Whatever Billings had was an international affair. The underworld of two continents was breaking out the war drums. We knew something was developing but we didn't know why, where or how."

"And how far are you now?"

The smile he gave me was cold. "In our own way we have made progress." I waited and smiled back, just as cold. If he wanted anything, then he couldn't afford to stop. He knew it and said, "Coincidence is the killer of men."

"It's late for philosophy."

"Yes, it is. We know something about Spanish Tom and Lias. We can guess at what happened."

I swung at a wild one. "They overheard something they shouldn't've."

51

The swing connected and big man squinted at me. He nodded then went on. "A dock watchman remembered them drinking behind some bales of rags. It wasn't too uncommon and it was easier letting them sleep it off than fight them off so he just forgot it.

"Later he was pulled away by someone yelling for help in the water and it took about an hour to drag some dame out who apparently didn't want to go. She stalled as long as she could. Our guess is that it was a feint to get the watchman off so a plant could be made on the *Gastry*.

"We figure that sometime during the action, either Escalante or Lias overheard or saw what was going on and figured it for the usual smuggling bit and thought they could step into the play and make a fast buck for themselves."

"How could you confirm it?" I asked.

"At that time Spanish customs, acting with *Interpol*, cracked down hard on all points. Nothing was getting out by the usual routes and four big outfits were broken up. Still, traffic had to get through and it's well known that these operations all have emergency plans and in this case one went into effect. Whatever it was couldn't stay in Lisbon without being uncovered sooner or later so the *Gastry* became the transporter."

"Who was involved on board?"

"Nobody. These affairs are not of the moment. They're set up far in advance. Undoubtedly the *Gastry* was fitted with a hiding place a long time ago to be used when necessary and without anyone on board being the wiser. When in the other port another operative would remove the shipment by preconceived plan. These groups are pretty smart. They're big business. Even big government. We checked out every man on the *Gastry* so far and they're clean. Lias and Escalante were there by coincidence. Some time we'll strip the ship down and find out how it was done."

"That brings us to Billings."

The big man looked across the table at me, the question in his eyes a genuine one. "Do you know how, Irish?"

"I think so."

"Are you going to wait to tell me?"

"No." I let all the pieces come together slowly and began to fit them in place. I said, "Through a language association the two met a guy named Juan Gonzales. They mentioned what they had and wanted a buyer. Juan got greedy all of a sudden, I think. He knew he could buy for peanuts and sell big. Maybe the two knew what a good going price was and kept it fairly high. Anyway, Juan knew the guy with the loot who was looking for a touch. Billings had ten grand of ready money. He let Juan make the buy, probably on a partnership basis. Later he killed him and

ad the buy for himself. Juan was a scared lad. Maybe he knew
e was set up to be tapped off. Billings was scared too. The
riginal owners wanted possession and were going after it. Bil-
ngs couldn't run fast enough. They caught him. He went out
tting me hold the bag."

"Who was it, Irish? Who is Lodo?"

"Art died because he was about to find out. Lodo was the code
ame for the Mafia enforcer on the east coast here."

He didn't say anything. It didn't seem to register on him.

"It's important, isn't it?" I said.

"Maybe. The Mafia is a catchall term sometimes. It's still big,
ut sometimes is the patsy for other big outfits. We have leads
nto most of the Mafia sections and haven't heard of this angle
et."

"There's always something new," I told him. "Now . . . how
new was what I told you?"

"New enough. It's going to change our operation." He
aused, stared at me and rubbed his chin with his fist. "You left
ut some parts, Irish."

"Like what?"

"Why everybody wants you dead."

I let him see my teeth. "I wish I knew. When I do, I'll have
our Lodo, laddie."

"Maybe you've done enough right now."

He saw more teeth. "No no, daddy-o. Remember in the
eginning . . . that big bundle of bills? I want them. I got
lans."

"Care to talk about them?"

"No. But I will give you something to look at. Whoever wants
ne has my place staked out. Some of those boys you'd like to
ave and you can get them if you try putting a decoy into my
ad. It could prove real interesting."

"We know where they are. We even had it in mind. We were
here when the Etchings picked you up this morning."

My mouth must have hung open. "Damn," I said. "That was
a ride. Why didn't you move in?"

He shrugged casually. "I didn't call it because I knew you'd
ome out of the trap. By the way, where are they now?"

I played it just as casually. "Someplace in Jersey and Stan
Etching has a hole in his gut."

"Fine," he said. "I'll put it down as a verbal report."

He stood up and said, "Be careful tonight. If you need help,
ou can call."

"Sure," I said. "Sure."

It was 3:35 and the day hadn't changed yet. I waited in the
loorway until a cab showed with his toplight on and I flagged
him down. I rode up to where the *Peter J. Haynes III Co., Inc.*

was out of sight 16 floors up and gave the business to the elevator boy. He looked at me, shrugged and sent the car up.

The place was quiet. From some distant room came the soft clack of a typewriter and from another angle there was the mute monotone of someone on the telephone. An unmarked door beside the reception desk opened and the redhead came out, saw me and grinned all over. She was in tight green and knew what it was doing for her. "I could hope you came to see me but I know you didn't."

"How come you work on Saturdays?"

"Only some Saturdays. It's quiet then and on busy seasons you can catch up."

"I get the kick. Carmen here?"

"Miss Smith?"

I shook my head. "Carmen. We're buddies."

Her eyes flicked away, then came back annoyed a moment before the smile touched them again. "Second best. That's how I always come out. No, she's not here. She was shopping and was in and out a couple of times. Did you call her home?"

"Uh-uh."

She reached for the phone and dialed a number. I heard it ring about half a dozen times then the redhead said, "Nobody's there, but do you want to leave a message?"

I didn't get it and she caught my look. She reached behind her head and slid a wall picture to one side. There, built in, was a tape recorder with half-filled spools. "Cuts in after the tenth ring," she said. "Canned voice asks for a message and you're free to talk for three minutes. Besides, they record all outgoing calls. Shall I leave a message?"

"Clever," I said. "So tell her I'll be there for supper at six." I heard the flat enunciation of the canned secretary, then the message was passed on.

When she hung up the redhead said, "Tell me, Mr. . . ."

"Ryan."

". . . Mr. Ryan . . . you're not going to hurt . . . Miss Smith are you?"

"I don't get it."

"She has lights in her eyes."

I waited for the rest of it.

She said, "I know who you are, Mr. Ryan. Although the pictures in the papers hardly flatter you."

I could feel myself go warm with a flash that only fear can start. Like a jerk I left myself wide open and this kid could put a damper on the whole thing. Maybe she saw what I was thinking. It should have been plain enough.

She smiled again. There was no malice, no guile in it at all. "I'm concerned about Miss Smith. Does she know?"

54

"She knows. She's helping out."

"You didn't do those things?"

"Some of them," I told her without hesitating. "They were justified. I think in the end it'll all come out clean."

"Think?"

"If I get knocked there'll be no washday, sugar. I'll be all dirty socks and bad memories, no wash, just a burial like skunk-sprayed clothes."

For a short space the laughter left her eyes and she said seriously, "Don't let that happen, Mr. Ryan."

"I'll try not to," I grinned.

There were some packages Carmen had left there and I took them with me. In their own way they provided a good cover on the street. A guy with packages has a normal look about him.

By the time I reached Carmen's apartment it was a quarter to six and I took the back way in. I got off the service elevator and used the key she had given me. When the door opened some crazy low-beat jazz flowed out at me and I saw her dancing to it in the middle of the room.

I put the packages down, walked in and watched her. She was great. To that jangled sound she danced a sensuous dance that didn't match the beat, but fitted the mood perfectly. Her sweater was tight and black and her breasts were free beneath it. Under their lovely swelling the mesh stretched and the flesh tints made startling contrasts against the black. The skirt was a full thing, deeply maroon, and when she spun it mushroomed out, giving a brief glimpse of long legs, beautifully rounded. Very deliberately, almost professionally, she twisted fast, and the mushroom flattened for a single moment and you knew that like with the sweater, there was nothing else at all. She laughed at me across the room and I caught at the studded belt she wore and drew her convexly against me and tasted her mouth.

Her breathing was deep and fast and there was a bloom in her face. Her eyes were lit up like stars and she touched my cheeks with her fingers. "I've never felt like this before, Irish."

"I haven't, either."

"I wish this were . . . for real. That we weren't . . . looking for anyone."

"We'll do it again. Another time."

"All right. Shall we eat? I have steak."

"I want you."

"Later," she said.

You got to see these places to believe them. It was what somebody had done to an old building to get floor space in one room and at the far end built a platform for the band. The johns were

55

on either side, but you could smell them when you came in. Later, with sweat, gin and cheap perfume you wouldn't notice it, but early, they stank.

The guy at the door took the ticket and gave Carmen a double take. She went all the way with the act even to a mouthful of gum and a shoulder strap bag that was nothing more than a weapon. The robbers inside hadn't started up-pricing the soft drinks yet, waiting for the whiskey crowd to come in. All five pieces of the band were there, real gone already in a cloud of smoke. They were doing a soft cha-cha with closed eyes, not playing for anybody but themselves as yet.

I took Carmen into the dance, playing it snug right in front of the sax man. He winked down at us and let it moan low. In back of us, at the door, they were coming in fast, about three stags to every couple. It was a trouble night.

Saturday, rain, not enough dames.

I said, "You need any prompting?"

Her hair swirled to the tempo of the music. "I know what to say."

"Tell me."

"Alfredo Lias. Off the *Gastry*. I gave him money to buy me a watch overseas. He said he'd meet me here."

"And watch out for the wolves."

"I like wolves," she said.

At 10 the place was crowded. Only stragglers were still coming in. All sides of the room were lined with the stags, eyeing the women, cutting in on those they picked out. Roaming around like restless dogs were a half dozen big ones, stopping the fights that started and getting rid of the troublemakers.

I took Carmen to the soft drink concession and bought two ginger ales for a buck. Before she finished hers, a sleek-looking gook in sharp duds came over and without looking at me, asked her to dance. She glanced at me for confirmation and I said, "Go ahead, it'll be a rare experience."

The gook's face pulled tight, but he took her arm without speaking and melted into the crowd on the floor. The little guy tapped my arm and said, "Señor, be careful of that one. He did not come here just to listen to the music."

I waited until they came around again and when the gook protested, I poked my finger in his eyeball and we walked away. In back the guy screamed into his hands.

We asked around and neither of us found the one we were looking for. At midnight they drew for the door prize and some dame won a bottle of Scotch.

At one the band was looking at their watches and two good-sized fights had broken out across the room. The bouncers took care of them in a hurry and a few were hustled out lengthwise. Couples had started to leave and even the ranks of the stags were thinning out. If Lias knew his friend was dead it wasn't likely that he'd be in a gay mood. If he were anywhere he'd be on the fringe of the crowd, taking advantage of numbers.

I sent Carmen into the ladies' john to see what she could find and began to tour the stags. Most of them were in bunches, talking, arguing, drinking and all the while thinking they were having a good time. I went all around the room without seeing anyone I'd tag as Lias, then I stopped for a Coke again. Carmen had been gone quite a while and I searched for her in the crowd, trying to pick her out of the mess. The guy with the apron full of money said, "You lose your gorl, señor?"

Without thinking I said, "No . . . my friend. Alfredo Lias. He's off the *Gastry*."

" 'Fredo? He was just here. He walk right behind you with that Maria." He stood on his toes and craned his neck, then shot his finger out. "See him, there he is, señor!"

I pretended to look, missing the direction. The guy said, "There, señor, the grey suit, by the empty soda boxes."

"I see him. Thanks."

"Sure, señor."

I crossed the floor, picking my way through the couples who were applauding the band. I looked at the sax man taking a bow and Carmen grabbed my arm. I pushed her ahead of me weaving through the groups.

"Ryan . . . he's here! A girl said he's with Maria and . . ."

"I know it, kid. There he is right there." I pointed to him and just then the band started another cha-cha-cha. I folded her into my arms and danced toward the one called 'Fredo. Before I reached him he stepped out onto the floor with the pretty black-haired girl and began to lose himself in the maze.

But he didn't lose me. I steered Carmen closer and then there he was, looking down at the girl Maria without really seeing her at all. His face was a mask that hid another face that was pure terror.

We moved in close until I was standing beside him. I said, " 'Fredo . . ." and the white of fear blanched the tan of his face and when his eyes met mine they were sick to death.

I made with a laugh, old friends meeting again, forced a handshake on him and herded us all outside the dance square. I told Carmen to take Maria and powder their noses while we said hello and when they left put my arm around the guy and for everyone's benefit who wanted to look did a palsy bit that went over all the way.

But not with Alfredo Lias. His eyes came up to mine, deep

57

and black. For some time now he had been living with this and now he thought it was here.

"You will keel me now, señor?"

I talked through a laugh and motionless lips. He was the only one who heard it. "I want you out of this mess, mister. I'm the only chance you got to get out, understand?"

He didn't but he said, "Si!"

"First we got to talk. You been here before?"

"Si. Often we come here."

"Anything out back? We have to talk somewhere."

His hand was like a talon around my forearm, hope giving him new life again. "By the corner is a door. Our back is where the garbage is put. Señor, they will kill me, no?"

"I hope not, kiddo. You go back there. I'll tell the girls to stay put and cruise on out."

"Si! I go. I tell you anything."

He walked away and angled across the dance floor. I waited beside the johns until Carmen and Maria came out then told them to hang on. Neither asked any questions. They seemed glad to talk.

I cut across in front of the bandstand where they started the next number. Halfway across I stopped and stared at the guy dancing with the tall, raven-haired doll. I said, "Hi, kid."

Jake McGaffney looked at me and said, "What're you doing here, Irish?"

"What about you?"

He grinned at the doll. "Hell, ask Bets here. She drags me to all these damn native affairs."

The doll smiled, said something to me in Spanish and danced off with Jake.

I got across to the other side, behind two kids wheeling out cardboard containers of refuse. The first one pulled at the door and while it was all the way open the night was split apart by the slamming reverberations of three close shots and right behind it every girl in the place began to scream her lungs out.

There was one mad rush for the front exits and curses spit out in a dozen different languages. Up front they clawed their way to the street over one another, knowing full well what those blasts meant. The two kids had jumped off like startled rabbits leaving the container wedged in the doorway and I had to climb over it to get outside.

My hand was tight around the butt of the .45 and I sucked myself into the shadows. I waited a full minute, but it didn't matter at all. Whoever fired the shots had gone.

But I wasn't alone. The small sound came from behind the stacked soda crates and I saw the dull grey of his suit and the contrasting brown of his face. He was almost white now. He had

58

one hand across his stomach and he had no reason to be alive at all.

I knelt beside him, the gun still in my hand. He saw it, but I shook my head. "I didn't do it, 'Fredo."

His voice was a harsh whisper. "I know . . . señor."

"Did you see him?"

"No. He was . . . behind me. I thought . . . it was you."

"Look, I'll get you a doctor . . ."

His hand touched my arm. "Señor . . . please, no. It is too late. I get bad. Now I pay. Like Tom. I pay. It is better."

I didn't argue with him. I said, "You know what you took from the ship?"

He nodded, his eyes half closed.

"What was it, 'Fredo?"

A hiccup caught at his chest and I knew there were only seconds left. "Eight . . . kilos . . . señor," he whispered.

Then I knew what it was all about. I wanted one last confirmation. " 'Fredo . . . listen. Juan talked you into selling to Billings?" His nod was weak and his eyes closed. "Somehow you heard about Lodo. All of you knew about Lodo?"

I put my ear close to his mouth. "We . . . are all . . . dead men . . . señor."

"Billings had the eight kilos last then?"

Another whisper. "Si."

" 'Fredo . . . who is Lodo?"

There was nothing more he could say.

From outside you could hear the sirens and the voices, and more sirens and more voices. They were getting louder and I couldn't wait. I went over the fence the way the killer had gone and like the way a city-bred animal can, found my way back to the open street and the safety of the night and the rain.

I had to show the cabbie the money before he'd take me back. He let me off where I asked and I found Pete-the-Dog selling his papers on the ginmill beat. I took him outside, bought all of his sheets for a couple minutes talk and got what I wanted. Some unknowns had brought action into the block. Somebody shilled Golden into popping off and he was dead. Holmes was in an emergency ward with a couple of slugs in his chest and not expected to live. Steckler was picked up on an assault charge against Razztazz and to top it a Sullivan Act violation which kicked his parole out and he was due in the big house for the rest of his stretch. Razz was okay. A little beat, but okay. I gave Pete his papers back and started back to the house.

The womb.

The familiar pattern, I thought. That's all a hood had was his house. His womb. You die in sleep. Each awakening was a birth. It was something precious, something you couldn't take away.

There hadn't been time to find Carmen, but I knew, somehow, that she'd be all right. Tomorrow I'd see her. Tomorrow.

I walked down the street paying no attention to the rain at all. It slashed down at me, the wind giving it a sharp bite. I held my head up and let it lick at my face. The stinging sensation had a cleansing, astringent effect and I thought over all the things that had happened. Not just tonight. All the other nights. There didn't have to be any more looking because I knew I had all the pieces. They were there. They would just take a little sorting out in the morning and I'd have the whole picture. Then the money. Then Carmen. Then life.

I opened my coat, held the .45 in my hand while I fumbled my key out. I shouldn't've bothered because the door was already open. I took my hat off, held it while I felt my way to the living room and flipped on the switch.

Even before the first blossom of light filled the room I remembered what was wrong. Pete-the-dog hadn't mentioned one name Mario Sen.

And here he was waiting for me to come in the door and his gun was leveled right at my stomach. He waited to let me see him smile his killer's smile and it was a smile too long. He never noticed the .45 in my fist under the hat I was holding and my first slug blew his brains all over the wall. The cordite and blood stink rushed into the room and for the first time I felt a little sick.

Out in the kitchen I let the water run until it was cold, took a long drink to wash the bitterness away that stained my mouth and went to the phone. I dialed the Big Man's number and when he came on I said, "This is Ryan. I found Lias. He's dead."

"I heard the report."

"He wasn't dead when I reached him, Big Man."

The intake of his breath made a sharp hiss. "What was it?"

"Big Man . . . about how much would eight kilos of heroin be worth on the final cut?"

He tried to keep the excitement out of his voice but couldn't make it. "That's way up in the millions. There hasn't been a single shipment that size in twenty years!"

"That's what was in your package mister. That's why everybody died."

"Have you located it?"

"Not yet. But I will."

"If you had a tail on Billings all the while, where did he hang around?"

"Hold on."

I heard a file drawer slide open, the rustle of papers, then the drawer slam shut. He picked up the phone again. "His movements were pretty well regimented. Mornings at the Barkley for

reakfast and a shave, on to the Green Bow or Nelson's, several
ars in the Forties and generally into the Snyder House for a
ard game at night. Just before he was killed he made two trips
o where the city's planning that new Valley Park Housing
Development. Walked around the block, but that was all."

"Those buildings are going to be torn down," I said.

"In a few months. There are still some families there yet."

"I know," I said.

"Any help?"

"Yes. Yes. Lots of help. Meantime you can pick up another
ead man at my place. His name is Mario Sen. He won't be
nissed. He was planted here to get me and you guys passed him
ver. I took care of it myself." I paused, then added, "I'll call you
back."

I hung up the phone while he was still trying to talk and sat
lown. It made lots of sense now. I knew what Billings was doing
n that old section. I had an apartment there for 10 years and he
ound out where. He was going to plant the stuff in my pad be-
ore he died and let it go from there.

The only thing he didn't know was that I had just moved out!

I reached for the phone again, held my hand on it and thought
back, all the way back to the beginning and ran it up to date.
There was no more puzzle then. The pieces became a picture
nd faces and times and events and now there was nothing left to
ind out at all . . . except for one thing.

All the tiredness left me and I felt good again, like that day in
he beginning. The sucker trap was over and I was out of it and
after tonight there wouldn't be a kill list at all. Not for me. For a
ot of others, maybe, but not me.

I grabbed at the phone, rang Carmen's number and she had it
before it finished ringing the first time. Her voice almost cracked
with anxiety when she said, "Ryan, Ryan, where are you?"

"Home, Baby, I'm okay. What happened?"

"We left with the rest. The police came up as I came out but
here weren't enough to catch us. We heard those shots and I
hought it was you. I couldn't get over there. It was like being
caught in the tide. Everybody was screaming and pressing
forward . . ."

"You can forget it now."

"Who was it?"

" 'Fredo. They got him."

"*Oh, Ryan.*"

"He was alive when I got there. He talked, kitten, and now I
can really twist some tails. You want to see it happen?"

"Only . . . if I can help."

"You can. Look, grab a cab and come over here, I'll be waiting
outside. We can go on from here." I gave her my address, hung

up and went in and changed my shirt. I walked past Mario Se
to the street and stood in the shadows, waiting.

When the cab stopped I got in and there was my lovely Car
men. Her breath half-caught in a relieved sob. She said my nam
and buried her face against my neck. I gave the driver my ol
address.

The street was dying. What life it had left showed in the fev
windows glowing a sickly yellow. Only a handful of kids mad
noises under the street lights. The plague it had even seemed t
reroute traffic which hurried by as if anxious to get away fror
the old and decaying.

I stopped, and Carmen looked up at me quizzically, her han
tight on my arm. "Thinking?"

"Reliving a little."

"Oh?"

"I used to live here." I nodded toward the blank row of win
dows that faced the second floor.

A thin stoop-shouldered old man, his face gaunt under th
grey velvet of a beard, shuffled out of the darkness, glanced at u
suspiciously, then twisted his mouth into a grin. "Evenin', M
Ryan. You come back for a last look?"

"Hi, Sandy. No, just a little unfinished business. How com
you're still here?"

"That Kopek Wrecking outfit got a bunch of us around. Sup
posed to keep out sleepers. You remember when they knocke
down that place with them two bums holed up inside? Cost then
for that."

I motioned toward the hallway on my right. "Anybody here?"

"Steve. He'll be drunk. You want to see him?"

"Not specially."

He flipped an off beat salute and said, "Well, have fun. Can'
see why anybody'd come back here. Three more weeks every
body's out and down they come."

We watched him walk off and Carmen said, "Sad little man.

I took her arm and we went up the time worn brownston
steps into the open maw of the tenement.

The scars of occupancy were still fresh, the *feel* of people stil
there. The pale light of the unshaded bulb overhead gave a fals
warmth and cast long, strange shadows around us. From some
where in the back came a cough and the mumble of a voice thic
with liquor.

A box-like professional torch with *Kopek Wrecking* stencile
on it was wedged in the angle between the bannister and th
newel post. I picked it up and snapped on the switch. Then
smiled at Carmen, took her hand and started up the stairs.

At the door I stopped and turned her head toward mine. "Yo
haven't said anything."

Her eyes laughed at me. She waved her hand at the darkness outside the light. "What can I say? Everything is so . . . strange." An involuntary shiver seemed to touch her and she drew closer to me. "The things you do . . . are so different. I never know what to expect."

"They're hood things, kitten."

For a moment she seemed pensive, then she shook her head lightly. "You're not really, Ryan. In the beginning you were, but something's happened to you."

"Not to me, sugar. Nothing in this whole lousy world is going to shake me up. I like being a hood. To me it's the only way I can tell off this stupid race of slobs. I can keep out of their damned organizations and petty grievances and keep them away from me. I can drink my own kind of poison and be dirty mean when they want me to drink theirs."

I tried the knob. It turned easily and the door opened.

In a way it was like visiting your own tomb.

There was my chair by the window. The drop leaf table Mrs. Winkler gave me was still in its usual position by the wall. Somebody had stolen the mirror and the magazine rack. When I turned the light into the bedroom the framework of the iron bed made a grilled pattern in shadows on the wall. Somebody had swiped the mattresses too.

I walked to the window and looked out into the street. The haze of dirt put things out of focus. I turned the head of the torch ceilingwise and put it on the floor, then sat down in the armchair.

Almost softly I said, "It's a 'once-upon-a-time' story. It started in Lisbon where two drunks named 'Fredo and Spanish Tom accidentally witnessed the caching of a narcotics shipment. In cubic displacement it only made a small package, eight kilos worth, but in value a multi-million dollar proposition. They never realized the full value of it. A few grand was as far as they could think.

"But others knew what it meant. In port they contacted a Spanish speaking buddy, Juan Gonzales. He knew a guy who had the loot to make the buy. That takes us to my old friend Billings. The louse."

For some reason I didn't feel the quick flush of hate I used to feel when I thought of his name.

"Juan made the buy for Billings, all right, and probably before he could pass over the ten grand he paid for it to Tom and 'Fredo, they shipped out. Juan didn't care for ten grand . . . you see, he was going to be Billings' partner in something really *big*. He even told his wife the great things they'd do . . . things you don't do on only ten grand.

"And now the rub. Billings didn't want a partner. The big

cross was coming up and Juan could feel it. He didn't have a chance in the world and he protected his wife the only way he could. He gave her that ten grand then tried to skip out. He didn't get far. Billings was waiting. He shoved him under a truck and that took care of Juan. He didn't worry about the other two since they never knew who made the buy."

The curiosity in her eyes deepened. Her tongue made a slight movement between her teeth as she followed my thought. She said, "But those other two . . . they're dead."

"I know. I'll come to that."

"Billings put eight kilos of junk on the market. I can't figure how he could have been so incredibly stupid, but apparently his greed got the better of him. *Eight kilos!* This was the biggest load that ever hit the states in one piece!"

I stopped a moment, thought about it, then said reflectively. "You know, this was what they were waiting for."

"They?" She was perched on the edge of the dropleaf table, her hands folded under her breasts making them strain against the fabric of the raincoat.

"*They*, sugar. Whenever eight kilos of H gets away from its handlers there's some hell waiting for somebody. An organizational hijacking they could cope with, but not coincidence. They didn't know where it was, but they knew it would show up in time. When it did they went after it and Billings was their target. The slob got smart too late.

"When the word went out how hot the junk was nobody would touch it. There were no buyers. That's when Billings knew he was about to be tapped. He tried to protect himself by going to a policing agency, but again it was too late. The stakes were too high. They knocked off his protection, moved in close and were ready to tap him out.

"Buddy Billings made his final move. He knew they wanted the stuff as well as him, so like he had done once before, he included me in the mess. Hell, he knew where I lived. He wanted me dead or imprisoned . . . anything to pay for the anxiety I had made him live with all the days I had hunted for him."

I stopped, sucked in a deep breath and looked at the ceiling patterns again.

"He hid the junk in my place, kid. He probably figured on writing an anonymous letter or something but they caught up with him beforehand. He wasn't quite dead when a cop found him. His last words implicated me.

"Now catch this. By now the underworld has been rattling with this story. The policy agency involved have a good picture of what they're after. This stuff has to be found before the original owners get it and put it into circulation.

"The catch, kiddo. They have two names. Mine, and a certain

Lodo. The last one is a killer. The head of operation kill. The wheel that Mafia HQ keeps set up to enforce its east coast programs and keep things in line. Lodo is rarely called upon, that's how clever the organization is, how big it is, how tightly it can work within the frameworks of certain governments. Narcotics are big . . . and legal . . . businesses in several countries. Lodo is an important cog in the machine . . . and Lodo is only a cover name.

"Lodo must be smart, untouchable, able to operate without suspicion. And now Lodo is responsible for recovery of eight kilos of H."

She began to see what I was driving at. "And all that time it was . . . at your place?"

"That's right."

She looked around quickly. "Here?"

I nodded. "Billings' mistake. He didn't know about the move."

"All that . . . is here?"

"I could almost say where."

She waited, her face reflecting her interest. I got up, went to the kitchen and in the barren limits of the light felt for the obvious wall partition by the sink that opened onto a series of valves. I hauled the carton out and shut the partition. My arm hit a cup that still stood on the sink and it crashed to the floor.

In the living room I heard Carmen gasp.

I put the carton beside the torch and sat down. "There was no other place in this dump to hide anything," I said.

The box fascinated her. I tapped it with my foot. "Eight kilos. Millions. Not one or two. Not ten. More than that. Enough to get a whole city killed off."

"It . . . doesn't seem like much," she admitted.

"It never does."

"And you found it. Nobody else could. Just you." Her voice held a touch of admiration and she was smiling.

"There were red herrings. Money Billings won on the nags. The fuzz thought it was loot I paid him for the stuff. *You know, all that time they sucked me in thinking I had possession and were trying to get it out of me. They knew I had to play their little game or else.*"

"Game?"

"Sure, sweetie. In my own crazy way I'm a fuzz too. They played the game to the hilt. They played it two ways at once and played it smart. I was the complete unknown and they didn't know what to do with me. What they pulled might be called the Ultimate Stunt. I like that. It fits real well. But what I like best is what I told them in the beginning. I was right. I was bigger than their whole damn department. Hoodtown's my back yard too and the game is my game as much as theirs. If I felt like it I could bust this play open like a ripe egg. Alone."

I said suddenly, "What made you do it, Carmen?"

She frowned and asked the question silently.

"Take the job, I mean."

"Job?"

"*Lodo*," I said softly. "*My beautiful big lovely is Lodo.*"

Her breath came in a gasp. "Ryan!"

"I'm going to guess again, kid. Check me. You probably never have before. But look deep. Look at a kid brought up around the gaming tables whose ears catch talk and intents kids shouldn't hear. Look at a kid who gets used to wrong money young, who learns the mechanics of card handling from an expert and who finds a taste for those things develop into a lust for them."

The next thing I let come out slowly.

"Look at a kid who blew a guy's head off from ten feet away and think of what impact that had on a mind already decaying."

For a moment a terrible shudder touched her shoulders and the beauty of her face was twisted with anguish.

"Stop it, Ryan! These things you're guessing . . ."

I shook my head. "I'm not guessing any more, kitten."

Her teeth bit into her lip and the tears that made her eyes swim flooded out and coursed down her cheeks.

I said, "Lodo left a line to Billings . . . a slim one, a deliberate one. Lodo had to maintain that connection to be in on things if they ever developed, yet not enough to be suspicious. That line was the sweet bouquet you sent the departed. The eventuality paid off. *I* followed it.

"Your next move was easy. On our first lunch date you went to the ladies room as per usual, but made a phone call that had me tailed. You made all the provisions for a tap job in my own apartment using organization punks and sat back and waited."

"Ryan . . ." her eyes were pleading, "do you think I *could* do that?"

"Sure. The kill wasn't yours directly. You just made the call. Operation tappo went into effect automatically. Trouble was, it didn't come off. The big second phase began. I was cultivated for information. I was still an enigma. Nobody could figure my part in it at all. Hell, don't feel sorry about it, I didn't know either."

She shook her head, telling me it was wrong, all wrong, but I didn't watch.

"My friend Art died before I could catch on. He had some great connections, that guy. They went pretty far. He was a big hero in the Italian campaign during the war. He made a lot of friends over there. He called on one to do some poking for him. He found out Lodo was a cover name and was about to find out who Lodo was. So Art had to die.

"Coincidence entered the picture again. You weren't deliberately set up for it . . . the gimmick was just there, that's all."

"Gimmick?" Her voice was quiet, her face expressionless.

"The tape recorder attachment on the phone. One in the office, one at home. You picked up my conversation with Art, went to his place and while he was asleep, killed him yourself or had him killed."

"No!"

I shrugged. "It really doesn't matter who did it. I prefer thinking it was you. By this time your organization had run down the Lisbon kids. One was bumped, one to go. The game was all yours when I figured when the last one would be. You had your stooges there and waiting and when the contact was made they beat me to the guy and the tap cleaned up that end of things."

I leaned back in the chair and stretched out my feet. "Pretty quick now this outfit of yours will take plenty of lumps."

"Please, Ryan . . ."

"You suckered me, kiddo. I'm sore at the whole business now. I'm sore because when things were getting tight you called out the troops. I was on everybody's kill list. All the big ones were called in, guns from all over the country. Suddenly I'm thinking like fuzz and want the whole damn bunch slammed. Suddenly I know that for a change I can be useful. Suddenly I see that playing hood isn't the big thing after all because it's playing with the things I hate."

I took a big, deep breath. "And suddenly I'm hating those things especially hard because I started to be in love for the first time and now I don't know if it will ever happen again. Suddenly I have a terrible feeling like when I walked in the room here. It's all over. Everything's all over. The mistakes have all been made and now it's all over."

And then she showed me how the first part was wrong and the second right. The mistake still to go was mine in thinking I could get my rod out before she could move. I was wrong. It was about to be all over. In that I was right.

I could see the hole in the end of the hammerless automatic she pointed at my head. It was a fascinating thing, a bottomless black eye. I looked over it at Carmen's smile. It was strained at first, then relaxed.

She was still very beautiful.

"What would you have done, Ryan?"

I shrugged, gauging the distance between us. I'd make the try, all right, but it would be no use.

"You were right, you know." She tossed her head, making her hair swirl again. "The Peter Haynes Company is a front. Very legal, economically sound. A wonderful place to keep . . . other records. A good source of income to keep key personnel in funds and in style until their services are needed. My file of personal correspondence there would be very enlightening to a cipher expert, but completely meaningless to anyone else."

When I gave her a hard smile she said, "That one little fact could break and smash half of the whole organization."

And now it was too late.

"What would you have done, Ryan?"

"I don't know."

"Killed me?"

I didn't lie about it. "No."

"Being a hood never became you. The one act of turning me in would have justified you. You could have walked straight again. I think now you really want to."

"Two things would have happened. In this state, the chair . . . or with a good lawyer, permanently confined to a mental institution. I couldn't live that way. It would be better to be dead."

Her face softened and the light glinted on the wetness that lay along her cheeks. "Only you couldn't kill me, Ryan. Why?"

"What difference does it make?"

I could hardly make out her words. "It makes a difference."

"I told you. I was falling in love. I was a jerk. So now I pay for being a jerk. A whole lifetime I laugh at the idiots who get tied up in love knots and then it happens to me. Well at least I won't be hurting for long. I'm going to make you do it to me fast, kitten."

"Please don't." Her lip was tight in her teeth, choking something back. "Did you really love me, Irish?"

"Okay, kid, get the last laugh. Make it loud. It was true. You were the one. I loved you very much."

Inside my heart was slamming against my ribs because I knew it was coming and I didn't know whether it would hurt or not and I was scared. I looked at her and tried to see inside her mind but I couldn't get past the tears. For some reason she smiled and it was like before when I didn't know all the things I did now and when I could look at her and want and hope. Her eyes were soft and misty and in their depths saw what happened to her . . . saw the realization come, the analysis, the rejection of the future and the decision. I saw her suddenly love and give the only thing she had to give and with the yell still choked in my throat and before I could move to stop her she said, "I love you, man."

Then she folded her arms and turned the gun against her heart and said the same words again only this time they were shattered by the blast of the gunshot.

"KICK IT OR KILL!"

"KICK IT OR KILL!"

An old switcher engine pulled the two-car train from the junction at Richfield over the 12-mile spur into Lake Rappaho. At the right time the ride could have been fun because the cars were leftovers from another era, but now it was a damn nuisance. Coal dust had powdered everything, settling into the mohair seats like sand and hanging in the air so you could taste it. Summer was two months gone and the mountains and valleys outside were funnelling down cold Canadian air. There was no heat in the car.

Ordinarily, I wouldn't have minded, but now the chill made my whole side ache again under the bandage and I was calling myself an idiot for listening to that doctor and his wild ideas about me having to take a complete rest. I could have holed up just as well in New York, but instead I fell for the fresh air routine and took his advice about this place.

Lake Rappaho was the end of the line. A single limp sack of mail and a half dozen packages came off the baggage car as I stepped down from the last one.

On the other side of the platform, a black '58 Chevy with a hand painted *TAXI* on its door stood empty. I saw the driver, all right. He and a wizened old stationmaster were in the office peering at me like I was a stray moose in church. But that's mountain country for you. When you're out of season and not expected, everybody goes into a G.I. hemorrhage.

I waved my thumb at the taxi, picked up my old B-4 bag and the mailing tube I kept my split bamboo rod in, walked across the station to the car, threw my gear in the back seat, then got in front for the drive into Pinewood. It was another five minutes before the driver came out.

He opened the door on the other side. "Afternoon. You going to Pinewood?"

"Anyplace else to go?"

He shook his head. "Not for fifty miles, I guess."

"Then let's go there."

He slid under the wheel and kicked the motor over. In backing around the corner of the station he made a pretense of seeing my duffel in the back. "You going fishing?"

"That's the general idea."

"No fishing now, you know. Wrong season."

"It's still open, isn't it?"

He nodded. "For the rest of the month. But there's no fish."

"Shut up," I said.

It was a four-mile trip into the fading sun to Pinewood and he didn't say anything again, but every foot of the way his hands were white around the wheel.

Pinewood had a permanent population of 2,500. It lay where the valley widened on one end of Lake Rappaho, a mile and a half long and four blocks wide. The summer cabins and homes on the outskirts were long closed and what activity there was centered around the main crossroads.

The Pines Hotel stood on the corner, a three-story white frame building whose second-story porch overhung the entire width of the sidewalk.

I paid the cabby, grabbed my luggage and went inside.

The two big guys bordering the door waited until I had crossed the lobby and was at the desk. Then they came up and watched while I signed the register. The heavy one took my card from the clip and looked at it.

"Mister Kelly Smith, New York City," he said. "That's a big place for a whole address."

"Sure is." The clerk edged up from his desk with a small, fixed smile divided between the other two and me.

"I'll be here two weeks," I told him. "I want a room upstairs away from the sun and take it out in advance." I pushed a hundred dollar bill across the desk and waited.

"Like if somebody wanted to find you in New York . . ." the big guy started to say.

I snatched the card from his fingers. "Then you look in the phone book. I'm listed," I said. I was feeling the old edge come back.

"Smith is a common name . . ."

"I'm the only Kelly Smith."

He tried to stare me down, but I wasn't playing any games. So instead he reached out and picked up my C note and looked at it carefully. "Haven't seen one of these in a long time."

I took that away from him too. "The way you're going you'll never see one," I said.

The clerk smiled, his eyes frightened, took the bill, and gave me $16 back. He handed me a room key. "Two-nineteen, on the corner."

The big guy touched me on the shoulder. "You're pretty fresh."

I grinned at him. "And you're a lousy cop. Now just get off my back or start conducting a decent investigation. If it'll make you happy, I'll be glad to drop by your office, give you a full B.G., let you take my prints, and play Dragnet all you want. But first I want to get cleaned up and get something to eat."

He suddenly developed a nervous mouth. "Supposing you do that. You do just that, huh?"

"Yeah," I said. "Later maybe," and watched him go out.

When the door closed the clerk said. "That was Captain Cox and his sergeant, Hal Vance."

"They always pull that act on tourists?"

"Well, no . . . no, of course not."

"How many are in the department here."

"The police? Oh . . . six, I think."

"That's two too many. They pull that stunt on me again while I'm here and I'll burn somebody's tail for them."

Behind me, a voice with a cold, throaty quality said, "I don't know whether I want you here or not."

I glanced at the clerk. "Nice place you run here. Who is he?"

"The owner." He nodded to a hand-carved plaque on his desk. It read, Miss Dari Dahl, Prop.

She was a big one, all right, full breasted and lovely with loose sun-bleached hair touching wide shoulders and smooth, tanned skin.

"You haven't any choice, honey. I got a receipt for two weeks. Now smile. A lovely mouse like you ought to be smiling all the time."

She smiled. Very prettily. Her mouth was lush like I knew it would be and she hip-tilted toward me deliberately. Only her eyes weren't smiling. She said, "Drop dead, you creep," and brushed by me.

There was something familiar about her name. The clerk gave me the answer. "It was her sister who killed herself in New York last year. Flori Dahl. She went out a window of the New Century Building."

I remembered it then. It made headlines when she landed on a parked U.N. car and almost killed a European delegate about to drive off with a notorious call girl. The tabloids spilled the bit before the hush needles went in.

"Tough," I said, "only she oughtn't to let it bug her like that."

I had supper in White's restaurant. I had a table in the corner where I could see the locals filter in to the bar up front. The few who ate were older couples and when they were done I was alone. But everybody knew where I was. They looked at me often enough. Not direct, friendly glances, but scared things that were touched with some hidden anger.

My waitress came over with a bill. I said softly, "Sugar . . . what the hell's the matter with this town?"

She was scared, too. "Sir?" was all she could manage.

I walked up to the bar.

At 8 o'clock, Captain Cox and Sergeant Vance came in and tried to make like they weren't watching me. Fifteen minutes

later, Dari Dahl came in. When she finally saw me her ey
became veiled with contempt, then she turned away and th
was that.

I was ready to go when the door opened again. You could fe
the freeze. Talk suddenly quieted down. The two guys
tweedy coats closed the door behind them and walked up to th
bar with studied casualness. Their clothes were just the rig
kind, but on the wrong people because they weren't Madiso
Avenuers at all. One was Nat Paley and the bigger guy yo
called Lennie Weaver when you wanted to stay friends, but,
you had a yen for dying quick, you gave him the Pigface ta
Margie Provetsky hung on him years ago.

I felt that crazy feeling come all over me and I wanted to gri
but for now I kept it in. I pushed my stool back and that's
far as I got. The little guy who stormed in was no more than 2
but he had an empty milk bottle in one hand and he mouthed
string of curses as he came at Paley and Weaver.

Trouble was, he talked too much. He tried to spill it ou
before he cut loose. Lenny laced him with a sudden backhan
as Nat grabbed him, took the bottle away, and slammed him t
the floor.

He wasn't hurt, but he was too emotionally gone to do any
thing more than cry. His face was contorted with hate.

Lenny grunted and picked up his drink. "You crazy
kid?"

"You dirty bastard!" The words were softly muffled. "Yo
talked her into working for him."

"Get outa here, kid."

"She didn't have to work up there. She had a job. Yo
showed her all that money, didn't you? That's why she worke
She always talked about having that kind of money. Yo
bastards! You dirty bastards!"

When Nat kicked him, the blood splashed all over his shoe
and the kid just lay there. He twitched, vomited, and started t
choke. The only one who moved was Dari. She managed to ge
him face down and held him like that until he moaned softl
and opened his eyes.

She glanced up with those wild eyes of hers and said, "Sonn
was right. You're dirty bastards."

"Would you like a kick in the face too, lady?" Lennie aske
her.

For a second it was real quiet, then I said, "Try it, Pig
face."

He spun around and my shoe ripped his sex machine apar
and while he was in the middle of a soundless scream I grabbe
Nat's hair and slammed his face against the bar. He yelled
swung at me, and one hand tore into the bandage over my rib

74

nd I felt the punk draining right out of me. But that was his last
hance. I almost brained him the next time and let him fall in a
eap on the floor with his buddy.

I faked a grin at Dari, walked past the two cops at the table,
nd said so everybody could hear me, "Nice clean town you got
ere, friend," and went outside to get sick.

The window was open and I could see my breath in the air,
ut just the same I was soaked with sweat. When the knock
ame on the door I automatically said to come on in, not caring
vho it was. My side was one gigantic ball of fire and it was going
o be another hour before the pills I had taken helped.

There was no sympathy in her voice. The disdain was still
here, only now it was touched by curiosity. She stood there,
er stomach flat under her dress, her breasts swelling out, and I
emembered pictures of the Amazons and thought that she
vould have made a good one. Especially naked.

"Sonny asked me to thank you."

Trying to make my voice sound real wasn't easy. "No
rouble."

"Do you . . . know what you're doing?"

She paused.

"What do you want in Pinewood?"

"A vacation, kitten. Two weeks. I have to do it. Now, will
vou do me a favor?" I closed my eyes. The fire in my side was
uilding up again.

"Yes?"

"In my B-4 bag over there . . . in the side pocket is a bottle of
apsules. Please . . ."

I heard the zipper run back, then the sharp intake of her
preath. The gun she found in the wrong side pocket suddenly
ell to the floor with a thump and then she was standing over me
gain. She had the bottle in her hand.

"You're a damned drug addict, aren't you? That's the way
hey get without their dosage. They get sick, they sweat, they
hake." She poured the caps back in the bottle and capped it.
'Your act in the restaurant stunk. Now act this one out." With a
quick flip of her wrist she threw the bottle out the window and I
leard it smash in the street.

"You filth," she said and walked out.

It was three in the afternoon when I woke up. I lay there
panting and, when the sudden sickness in my stomach sub-
sided, I got to my feet and undressed. Outside, a steady light
rain tapped against the windows.

A hot shower was like a rebirth.

The .45 was still on the floor where Dari Dahl had let it drop and I hooked it with my foot, picked it up, and zippered it in side my leather shaving kit.

Every time I thought of that crazy broad throwing that bott out the window I felt like laying her out. That wasn't gettin those capsules back, though. I had maybe another two hours go and I was going to need them bad, bad, bad. I stuffed 50 buck in my pocket and went downstairs.

Outside my window, I found the remains of the bottle. Th capsules inside had long since dissolved and been washed awa by the rain.

I shrugged it off, found the drugstore and passed my spar prescription over to the clerk. He glanced at it, looked at m sharply, and said, "This will take an hour."

"Yeah, I know. I'll be back."

I headed for the restaurant. Although lights were on in stor fronts and the corner traffic blinker winked steadily, there wasn a car or a person on the street. It was like a ghost town.

The restaurant was empty. The waitress recognized me with peculiar smile, took my order, and half-ran to the kitchen. Th bartender walked across the room to me.

He was a graying man in his late 40s, a little too thin with dee tired eyes. "Look, mister," he said, "I don't want trouble i here."

I leaned back in my chair. "You know who those jokers were?"

He nodded. "We'll handle things our own way."

"Then start by keeping out of my hair, friend," I told him "I don't know how or why those punks are here, but they're th kind of trouble people like you just don't handle at all, so b grateful for the little things, understand?"

He didn't understand at all and his face showed it. He glance outside toward the distant slope of the mountain. "You aren' . . . on the hill?"

"Mac, I don't know what the hell you're talking about. think you people are nuts, that's all. I pull those punks off th kid's back last night while you, the cops, and everybody else just watch and *I* catch the hard time. I don't get it."

The door slammed open and Sergeant Vance came in. He came sidling over and tossed a sheet of paper down on the table. It was my prescription.

"This calls for narcotics, mister. You better come up with damn good explanation."

Real slowly I stood up. Vance was a big guy, but he wasn' looking down on me at all. Not at all. His face was all mean but scared too like the rest and his hand jumped to the butt of his service revolver.

I said, "Okay, you clown, I'll give you one explanation and if you ask again I'll shove that gun of yours up your pipe. That's a legitimate prescription you got there and, if you do any checking, you check the doctor who issued it first. Then, if it's bad, you come back to me. Meanwhile, you have a certain procedure to take that's down in black and white in the statute books. Now you take that prescription back and see that it gets filled or you'll be chewing on a warrant for your own arrest."

He got it, all right. For a minute, I thought I was going to have to take the rod away from him, but the message got through in time. He went out as fast as he came in.

What a hell of a vacation this was. Brother!

Willie Elkins, who owned a garage, was willing to rent me his pickup truck for 15 bucks a week. It was a dilapidated thing, but all I needed. He told me how to find old Mort Steiger, who rented boats. The old guy let me have my pick, then shook his head at me and grinned through his broken plate. "You ain't no fisherman, are you?"

"Nope," I shook back. "I try once in a while, but I'm no fisherman."

He paused, watching me warily. "You on the hill?"

"What is this 'hill' business? Who's up on what hill?"

He waited a moment, sucking on his lips. "You kiddin'? No, guess you ain't." He pointed a gnarled finger over my shoulder. "Big place up there just around that ridge. Can't see it from here, but she has a private road that comes right down to the lake, all fenced in. Whole place like that. You can't get in or out unless they let you."

"Who let's you?"

"City people. That's Mister Simpson's place. Big manufacturer of something or other. Never met him myself. He likes it private."

I let out a grunt. "He sure does. He has a real goon squad working for him. I met a couple last night. They needed straightening out."

This time his grin got broader and he chuckled. "So you're the one. Willie told me about that. Could be you'll make trouble for yourself, you don't watch out."

"It won't come from two-bit punks, pop. Trouble is, if Simpson's such a big one, what's he doing with guys like that on his place?"

"Maybe I could tell you."

I waited.

"This Simpson feller was a big one long time ago. Bootlegging or something, then he went straight. He had all this money so he went into business. Few times a year he comes up here, does some business, and leaves."

"Everybody in town is scared, pop. That's not good business.

His eyes seemed to scratch the ground. "Ain't the business h
does."

"What then?"

"The girls. He sends down to Pinewood for girls."

"The place looks big enough to support a few hookers."

"Mister, you just don't know country towns. Comes end o
summer and *those* girls pack up and leave. It's the others h
gets."

"Listen, a guy that big wouldn't try . . ."

He interrupted with a wave of his hand. "You got me wrong
He . . . employs them."

"Well, what's wrong with that?"

"They go up there, all right, but they don't come back . .
well, the same . . . Rita Moffet and the oldest Spencer gi
moved over to Sunbar. Bob Rayburn's only girl, she neve
would speak to anybody and last year they had to send her t
the State Hospital. She still won't speak to anybody at all. Flo
Dahl and Ruth Gleason went off to New York. Flori died ther
and nobody has heard from Ruth in months."

"Nice picture."

"Others, too. That's not all. Some are still here and ever
time Simpson and the bunch comes in they go up there to work
Like they enjoy it. He pays them plenty, oh, you can bet that
What stuff they buy, and all from New York."

"Any complaints?"

The old man frowned. "That's the funny part. None of 'em
say nothing."

I stood up and stretched. "You know what I think? Thi
Simpson guy pays them mighty generously and for the firs
time they get a look at how the other half lives and want to give
it a try. So they leave town. It's an old story. The others won'
leave, but let the gravy come to them. How about that?"

"He got funny people working for him. They bring trouble t
town, mister."

"Okay, so he hires hoods. I know reputable businessmen wh
have done the same."

Steiger thought it over. "Maybe, but did you ever see such a
scared town in your life, mister?"

The drizzle had stopped. I zippered up my jacket and shoved
my hat on. Mort Steiger watched me carefully.

Finally he said, "You're a funny one, too, mister."

"Oh?"

"You got a real mean look. You're big and you look mean.
You tell me something true?"

I opened the door of the pickup and said over my shoulder,
"Sure I'll tell you true, pop."

78

"You ever kill anybody?"

I slammed the door shut and looked at him. He was completely serious.

Finally I nodded. "Yes. Six people."

"I don't mean in the war, son."

"I wasn't talking about the war."

"How'd you do it?"

"I shot them," I said and let the clutch out.

The druggist had my prescription ready and handed it over without a word. I knew he had checked on the doctor who issued it and had another check going through different channels. I ordered a Coke, took two of the capsules, and pocketed the rest.

A fresh rain slick was showing on the street and the weather forecast was that it would continue for a few days. So I'd fish in the rain. I'd take a six-pack of Blue Ribbon and a couple sandwiches along and anchor in the middle of the lake under an umbrella.

I went outside, flipped a mental coin to see where I'd eat. The coffee shop in the hotel won and I hopped in the truck. At the corner the blinker was red on my side and I rolled to a stop. As I did, a new black Caddy with Kings County (New York) plates made the turn and I had a fast look at the driver.

His name was Benny Quick, he had done two turns in Sing Sing on felony counts and was supposedly running a dry-cleaning place in Miami. There was somebody beside him and somebody in the back, but I couldn't make them out.

I made a U turn, passed the sedan, turned right two blocks farther on, and let the Caddy pass behind me. That's all I needed to pick up the license number. A friend back in New York would do the rest.

I couldn't figure what Benny Quick was doing up this way, but I made a living being nosy and I had been too long at it to let a vacation take me out of the habit.

Back at the Pines Hotel, I shared the coffee shop with a half dozen teen-agers sipping coffee and feeding the juke box. None of them paid any attention to me. The waitress snapped the menu down in front of me.

When I looked up I said, "You ought to smile more, Miss Dahl."

"Not for you, Mr. Smith."

"Call me Kelly."

She ignored me completely and waited. I told her what I wanted, and while I waited scanned a newspaper. The headlines were still all about Cuba.

79

Dari Dahl came back, fired my cheeseburgers at me, and put the coffee down so hard it spilled. I said, "Go back and get me another cup."

"What?"

"Damn it, you heard me. I've had about all the crap from you I can take. You be as sore as you please, but, baby, treat me like a customer or for kicks I'll throw these dishes through your front window. This town is giving me the business and from now on the business stops. Now shake your butt and get me another coffee and do it right."

The next time the coffee came slow and easy. I said, "Sit down."

She paused. "Mr. Smith . . ."

When I looked up and she saw my face, she grew chalky and pulled out a chair.

Dari Dahl was a magnificent woman, even scared. The tight nylon uniform outlined the daring cut of her underthings. The word bra was disputable for all that it was, and below it, far below, was a bikini-like thing beautifully discernible.

"I heard about your sister," I said.

"Let's not discuss it."

"Dari baby, it won't be too hard to find out someplace else. I remember the rough details. Any old newspaper account could fill me in. Anybody around town ought to be glad to talk about the bit."

The hardness came back again, her mouth pulling tight at the corners. "You should be able to understand it. My sister was a drug addict, when she could no longer supply her need, she killed herself. Eventually, you'll do the same."

"I will?"

"Your supposed legitimate source of supply through our druggist won't last very long. My sister used stolen and forged prescriptions, too, for a while. It was when they ran out that she killed herself." She stopped, her eyes glinting. "Tell me, Mr. Smith, are you here now because there are no other pharmacists who will honor your prescriptions? Is that it?"

Slowly, I finished my coffee. "You really are bugged, kid. You really are."

She walked away, tall, cool, a lovely, curvy animal, as beautiful as any woman ever was, but going completely to waste.

I left a buck and a half by my plate, went upstairs where I showered and changed into a city suit. I decided to try the air again. There should be a movie or a decent bar someplace.

I reached for the phone, but remembered the clerk downstairs and hung up. In the lobby, I called from a house phone where I could watch the desk, gave a New York number, and waited.

When my number answered, I said, "Artie?"

"Yeah, hi ya, Kelly, how's it going?"

For a full five minutes we made idle conversation about nothing, throwing in enough dirty words so any prudish operator bugging in would knock it off in disgust. Then I said, "Run a number through for me, kid, then get me all the information on its owner. Next, find out what you can about Benny Quick. He's supposed to be in Miami." I fed him the license number, talked a little more about nothing, and hung up.

Outside, the rain had started again, harder this time. I looked each way, saw a couple of recognizable lights, grinned, and walked toward them.

Like a whore's is red, police lights have to be green, old-fashioned, and fly-specked. You know from the sight of them what it's going to smell like inside. There's a man smell of wet wool, cigars, and sweat. There's a smell of wood, oiled-down dust; of stale coffee, and musty things long stored. On top of that, there's another smell a little more quiet, one of fear and shame that comes from the other people who aren't cops and who go down forever in the desk book.

I walked in and let Sergeant Vance stare at me like a snake and then said, "Where's your captain?"

"What do you want him for?"

The pair of young beat cops who had been standing in the corner moved in on the balls of their feet. They were all set to take me when the office door opened and Cox said, "Knock it off, Woodie." He ran his eyes up and down me. "What do you want?"

I grinned at him, but it wasn't friendly at all. "You wanted my prints, remember? You said to stop by."

He flushed, then his jaw went hard. He came out of the doorway and faced me from three feet away. "You're a rough character, buddy. You think we don't know what to do with rough guys?"

And I gave it to him all the way. I said, "No, I don't think you know what to do with rough guys, Captain. I think you're all yak and nothing else."

Across his forehead, a small pulse beat steadily. But he held it in better than I thought he could. His voice was hard but restrained when he told the beat cop behind me, "Take his prints, Woodie."

I gave him my name and address and stopped right there. If he wanted anything on me he could get it only after he booked me. I grinned at everybody again, left a bunch of stinking mad cops behind me, and went out into the fresh air.

It was 9 o'clock, too late for a show but not for a bar. I found one called JIMMIE'S with Jimmie himself at the bar and ordered a beer. Jimmie was a nice old guy and gassed with me.

When I finally got around to the Simpson place, he made a wry face and said, "Nobody ever saw the guy I know of. Not down here in town."

"How about the girls?"

He nodded. "You don't get much out of them. Simpson turns out to be either big or little, skinny or fat and you get the point. They don't talk it up any."

"So they don't talk about their boss. They get paid plenty, I hear."

"Hell, yes. Bonnie Ann and Grace Shaefer both sport minks and throw plenty of bucks around. Every once in a while I see Helen Allen in a new car. She comes through about once a month to see her folks. Used to be a nice kid. All of them were."

"Making money changed that?"

Jimmie shook his head, squinting. "No, but used to be they were plain hustlers and not high on anybody's list."

I asked, "You mean that's their job up there?"

His shrug was noncommittal. "They won't say. Some of them do secretarial work, answering phones and all that, because the switchboard operators here have talked to them often enough."

"If they're that interested, why doesn't somebody just ring Simpson's bell and ask?"

Jimmie gave a short laugh. "Besides the brush-off at the gate, who wants to spoil a good thing? Before that bunch leaves there'll be a bunch of money in this town, and off season you don't kick out found loot. Then there's another angle. That boy's a big taxpayer. He's got connections where they count, as some busybodies found out. A few local do-gooders tried some snooping and wound up holding their behinds. Nobody goes to the cops, though I can't see them doing much about it. Cox is like a cat who's afraid of a mouse yet getting hungry enough so he knows he has to eat one or die. I think he figures if he eats one it'll be poisoned and he'll die, too."

He opened me another bottle and moved on down the bar to take care of a new customer. It was the nervous taxi driver who tried to steer me away from Pinewood in the first place. I was beginning to wish I had let him talk me into it.

He ordered a beer, said something about the weather, then confidentially told Jimmie, "Saw somebody tonight. Didn't recognize her at first, but it was Ruth Gleason."

I poured my glass full, making like I was concentrating on it. Ruth Gleason was the girl Mort Steiger told me ran off to New York the same time Flori Dahl did.

"You sure?" Jimmie asked him.

"Oughta know her, I guess. She's changed though. She's got on fancy clothes and all that, but her face is sure old looking. Wouldn't look at me. She kind of turned away when she saw me."

"Well what's she doing back here?"

"Who knows? She got in that blue ranchwagon from the hill place and drove off." He waved off another beer and went out.

Jimmie came back wiping his hands on his apron.

Bluntly, I said, "Mort told me about the Gleason kid, too."

He didn't question my tone. "Nice girl. She was up there a whole month. Hardly ever came down and when she did she wouldn't speak to anybody. Flori and she went in at the same time. Flori used to come to town occasionally and the way she changed was hard to believe."

"How?"

He waved his hands expressively. "Like you can't pin it down. Just changed. They wouldn't look at you or hardly speak. It was real queer."

"Didn't any of those kids have parents?"

"Flori's old man was dying and they had no mother. I think Flori took the job up there to help get her old man into the Humboldt Hospital. They got him there, but he died soon after. Cancer."

"That's only one," I pointed out.

"Ah, who can tell kids anyhow? They do what they please anyway. Sure, some of them had folks, but there's big money up there."

He popped the top from another bottle and passed it over. "On the house." He took a short one himself, and we gave a silent toast and threw them down.

Then he said, "Better not do too much talking around town. This is a spooky place."

I grinned, paid off my tab, and waved him good night.

For a few minutes I stood under the awning watching the rain, then started back toward the center of town. I had crossed the street and almost reached the corner when the big Imperial came from my left, turned left, and stopped half a block up ahead of me. Unconsciously, I stepped into the darker shadows and walked faster.

Someone stepped out of the car, turned and pulled at another. They stood there together a moment and then I heard the unmistakable spasm of a sob.

I ran then, holding one hand tight against my ribs to muffle the fire that had started there. I was too late. They heard my

83

feet pounding and the one by the car turned sharply, ducked inside, and slammed the door. The car pulled away silently and slowly as if nothing had happened.

But they left a beautiful young girl behind them. She was sobbing hysterically and started to collapse as I reached her.

She was a lovely brunette wrapped tightly in a white trench coat, her hair spilling wetly over her shoulders. She tried to shove me away while she hung on desperately to an oversize handbag and kept saying over and over, "No . . . please, no!"

I said, "Easy, kid," and pulled her to the porch steps of the nearest house. When I got her seated I tried to take her hand. She stopped sobbing then, jerked her hand, and held her pocketbook on the opposite side.

For a second the hysteria passed and she said, "Get out of here. Let me alone!"

"Relax, I'm . . ."

"There's nothing the matter with me," she nearly shouted. "Get out of here. *Let me alone!*"

She clenched her teeth on the last word with a crazy grimace and tried to stand up. But I was sitting on one edge of her coat and when she did the thing yanked open and half-pulled off her shoulder.

She was naked from the waist up and I didn't need any light to see the welts and stripes across her body and the small bleeding spots where something with a sharp tip had dug in.

I stood up, pulled the trench coat closed. When she realized I had seen her, she closed her eyes, let out a soft, mewing sound, and let herself fold up in my arms. I put her down on the steps again and as I did, her pocketbook fell open. There was a sheaf of brand new bills inside, held by a bank wrapper. On it was printed the number 1,000.

Suddenly the porch light snapped on, the door opened, and a man stood there clutching his bathrobe at his middle. His wife peered over his shoulder, her face worried.

"You," he called out. "What are you doing there?" His voice didn't have too much snap to it.

I motioned to the girl. "There's a sick woman here. Look, call a doctor for me and hurry it, will you?"

"A doctor? What's . . ."

"Never mind what's the matter. You call. And turn out that light."

They were glad to get back inside. The porch light went out and inside one turned on. I propped the kid up, put her bag under her arm, and walked away from the house.

I didn't get very far. The car hissed up behind me and a voice said, "It's him again. The one who jumped Lennie and me in the restaurant."

There wasn't any sense running. A dozen fast steps would tear my side anyway. I just stood there and because I did the action that was all set to explode went sour. Nat Paley and the new guy who hopped out and came at me from different sides slowed, not able to figure me out.

Nat's hand came out of his pocket with a gun. The gun came up and Nat's face said it was the right time and the right place. Except somebody else thought differently and a strangely cold voice from inside the car said, "No noise."

They moved before I could yell. The other guy came in fast from the side, but I ducked in time to get the load in his fist off the top of my head. I kicked out, jabbed at his eyes, and made the touch. He couldn't yell with the sudden pain, ducked into my right and his face seemed to come apart under my knuckles.

And that was the end of it. Nat got me just right, one stunning blow behind the ear, and, as I sunk to my knees, went over me expertly with a clubbed gun and ruthless feet. As one terrible kick exploded into my side, I thought I screamed and knew with absolute certainty that Nat had one more blow to deliver. It would come with bone-crunching force in that deadly spot at the base of the brain. I knew it was coming and I hoped it would, anything that would erase the awful thing that was happening to me inside.

It came all right, but a sudden convulsion that wracked my side made it miss and my shoulder took it all. Nat didn't realize that, though. A tiny part of my mind that could still discern things heard him laugh and drag the other guy into the car.

In the middle of a wild dream of sound and light I coughed, tried to turn my head away from the jarring, acrid fumes of ammonia, and then swam back into a consciousness I didn't want.

Somebody had carried me to the steps and a face peered anxiously into mine. The old guy watching me said, "It's all right. I'm Doctor McKeever."

"The girl . . ." I started.

"She's all right. She's inside. We'd better get you in there, too."

"I'm fine."

"What happened? Was there an accident?"

I shook my head, clearing it. "No . . . not actually."

When I moved my arm my shoulder muscles screamed. At least nothing was broken. I'd taken some bad ones before, but this took the cake. Under the bandages I could feel the warmth of blood and knew what was happening.

I said, "You saw the girl?"

"Yes."

"You got an idea of what happened?"

He chewed his lips a moment and nodded. "I know."

"You've seen it before, haven't you?"

At first he wasn't going to say anything, then he looked at me again. His voice had an edge to it. "Yes."

"Then you do like you did before, doc. You keep this under your hat, too. Let it get out and that kid is ruined here in town. She can be ruined no matter where she goes and it isn't worth a public announcement."

"Somebody has got to stop it," he said.

I said, "It'll be stopped, doc. It'll be stopped."

A small frown furrowed his forehead. His smile was crooked. "Toxin-anti-toxin," he said.

"What?"

"Poison against poison."

I nodded, spit, and said, "You go take care of that kid, then ride me back to the hotel."

When he had left I got sick again. I had to get those capsules I had left in my room. In just a few minutes now it was going to be worse than it ever had been and I'd be a raving maniac without a big jolt from the small bottle.

I couldn't tell how long he had been gone, but finally he came out leading the girl. A car pulled around from the side and the doctor bundled her into it, telling the driver to take her to his office and deliver her to his wife.

As soon as the car left, he had me on my feet, got me in his Ford, and started up. At the hotel he got out, opened my door, and took the arm on my good side to lead me in.

Dari Dahl was behind the desk, in white nylon no longer. She was wearing a black sweater and skirt combination that dramatized every curve of her body and making the yellow of her hair look like a pool of light.

The brief flicker of concern that hit her face turned to a peculiar look of satisfaction. She came around the desk, tiny lines playing at the corner of her mouth and said, "Trouble?"

"What else. Now get my key, please."

She smiled, went back, picked the key out, and came over and handed it to me. "Are you hurting, Mr. Smith?"

Both of us shot her funny looks.

"Is it true that when a narcotic addict tries to lay off he fights it until he's almost tortured to death before he takes a dose?"

McKeever said, "What are you talking about, Dari?"

"Ask him." She smiled too sweetly.

"She's bugged, doc, let's go."

We walked to the stairs, started up them, when Dari called, "Mr. Smith . . ."

I stopped, knowing somehow what was coming.

"Quite accidentally I dropped a bottle of capsules while cleaning your room. They fell down the toilet." She stopped, letting it sink in, then added, "And so did several prescriptions that were with the bottle. I hope you don't mind too much."

She could see the sweat that beaded my face and laughed. I could hear it all the way up the steps.

I flopped on the bed and it was then, when my coat came open, that McKeever saw the blood. He opened my shirt, saw the red seeping through the bandages, took one look at the color of my face, and rushed out.

Lying there, my ribs wouldn't flex to my breathing and the air seemed to whistle in my throat. It was like being branded; only the iron never left.

The door opened and I thought it was McKeever back, then I smelled the fragrance of her across the room. My eyes slitted open. She wasn't wearing that funny smile she had before.

"What the hell do you want?" I managed to get out.

"Doctor McKeever told me . . ." she paused and moistened her lips, "about Gloria Evans. You tried to help her."

"So what?" I said nastily.

"You tried to help Sonny Holmes the other night, too."

"Sure, I'm everybody's buddy."

I closed my eyes, trying to control my breathing. She said softly, a still determined tone in her voice, "About the other thing . . . drugs. I'm not sorry about that at all."

McKeever came in then, panting from the run up the stairs. He uncovered me, got his fingers under the bandage and worked it off. He said, "A doctor took care of you, didn't he?"

All I could do was nod.

I smelled the flower smell of her as she came closer and heard the sharp intake of her breath as she saw me. "What . . . happened?"

"This man has been shot. He's recuperating from an operation." I heard Dr. McKeever open the bag and the clink of bottles. "Didn't you have anything to take periodically to kill the pain?"

I nodded again, my face a pool of sweat. I felt the needle go in my arm and knew it would be all right soon. I said through teeth held so tight they felt like they'd snap off, "Capsules. Morphine sulphate."

"*Oh, no!*" Her voice sounded stunned.

McKeever said, "What?"

"I thought he was a drug addict. I destroyed them."

The doctor said nothing.

Slowly the pain was lifting like a fog. Another second and I'd sleep.

Tonelessly, Dari said, "How he must hate me!"
Then I was past answering her.

It stopped raining on Wednesday. For two days I had lain
there listening to my bedside radio. The hourly news broadcasts
gave the latest U.N. machinations, then into the Cuban affair.
Now the finger was pointing at Cuba as being the new jumping
off place for narcotic shipments to the States. Under suspected
Soviet sponsorship, the stuff came in easily and cheaply from
China—a cleverly different kind of time bomb a country can use
to soften an enemy.

But two days were enough. I found my clothes, shaved,
dressed, and tried to work the stiffness out of my muscles. Even
then, the stairs almost got me. I took it easy going down, trying
to look more unconcerned than I felt.

McKeever wasn't glad to see me. He told me I had no business being up yet and told me to sit down while he checked the
bandage. When he finished he said, "I never asked about that
gunshot wound."

"Go on."

"I assume it has been reported."

"You assume right."

"However. I'm going to report it again."

"Be my guest, doc. To save time I suggest you get the
doctor's name from the prescription I had filled here."

"I will." He got up and reached for the phone.

The druggist gave him the doctor's name, then he called New
York. When the phone stopped cackling, McKeever nodded,
"It was reported, all right. Those prescriptions were good.
Then you really are here on . . . a vacation."

"Nobody seems to believe it."

"You've been causing talk since you came."

"What about the girl?" I said. "Gloria Evans."

He slumped back in his chair. "She's all right. I have her at
my wife's sister's place."

"She talk?"

The doctor shook his head. "No, they never talk." He took a
deep breath, tapped his fingers against the desk and said, "She
was badly beaten, but there was a marked peculiarity about it.
She was *carefully* beaten. Two instruments were used. One
appears to be a long, thin belt; the other a fine braided whip-like
thing with a small metal tip."

I leaned forward. "Punishment?"

McKeever shook his head. "No. The instruments used were
too light. The application had too deliberate a pattern to it."

"There were others like that?"

88

"I took care of two of them. It wasn't very pretty, but they couldn't talk. What happened to them would never leave permanent scars . . . but there are other ways of scarring people."

"One thing more, doc. Were they under any narcotic influence at all?"

McKeever sighed deeply. "Yes. The Evans girl had two syringe marks in her forearm. The others had them too, but I didn't consider them for what they were then."

I stood up. "Picture coming through, doc?"

He looked like he didn't want to believe it. "It doesn't seem reasonable."

"It never does," I told him.

I stopped at the hotel and took the .45 from my shaving kit. I checked the load, jacked one in the chamber and let the hammer down easy, then shoved it under my belt on my good side. I dropped a handful of shells in my coat pocket just in case. In the bathroom I washed down two of my capsules, locked my door, and went downstairs.

The clerk waved me over. "New York call for you, Mr. Smith. Want me to get the number back? It was paid."

I told him to go ahead. It was Artie on the other end and after helloing me he said, "I have your items for you, Kelly."

"Go ahead."

"One, the car belongs to Don Casales. He's a moderate-sized hood from the L.A. area and clean. Casales works for Carter Lansing who used to have big mob connections in the old days. Now he's going straight and owns most of So-Flo Airways with headquarters in Miami. Two, Benny Quick has left the Miami area for parts unknown. Benny has been showing lots of green lately. Anything else?"

"Yeah. Name Simpson in connection with Nat Paley or Lennie Weaver mean anything?"

"Sure, remember Red Dog Wally? He's got a bookie stall on Forty-ninth . . . other day he mentioned old Pigface Weaver. Some broad was around looking him up with tears in her eyes. A real looker, he said, but nobody knew a thing about Lennie. Red Dog said he'd ask around, found out that Lenny and Nat had something big going for them with an out of town customer and were playing it cozy. No squeal out on them either. So Red Dog told the broad and she almost broke down."

"Then their client could be Simpson."

"Who knows. Hell, they've strong-armed for big guys from politicians to ladies' underwear manufacturers."

"Okay, Artie, thanks a bunch."

I hung up and stood there a minute, trying to think. I went

over the picture twice and picked up an angle. I grinned at th
thought and turned around.

She was waiting for me, tall, beautiful, her hair so shiny yc
wanted to bathe in it. The gentle rise and fall of her breasts sai
this was a moment she had thought about and planned. Sh
tried a tiny smile and said, "Kelly?"

"Let's keep it Mr. Smith. I don't want to be friendly with th
help."

She tried to hold her head up and keep the smile on, but
saw her eyes go wet.

I tipped her chin up. "Now that we've exchanged nastie
everybody's even. Think you can smile again?"

It came back, crookedly at first, but there it was and she wa
something so damn crazy special I could hardly believe it.

"Mr. Smith . . ."

I took her hand. "Kelly. Let's make it Kelly, sugar."

Before I knew what she was going to do it was over, a kis
barely touching, but for one fraction of an instant a fierce, re
strained moment. We both felt it and under the sheer midnigh
of her blouse a ripple seemed to touch her shoulder and he
breasts went hard.

She went with me, out to the truck, waiting while I went int
police headquarters. I asked for Captain Cox and when he cam
said, "I want to lodge a complaint against two of Mr. Simpson
employees. One is Nat Paley, the other a stranger."

Cox's face drew tight. "About your brawl, I suppose."

"That's right. They attacked me on the street. I recognize
Paley and can identify the other by sight."

Nodding, Cox said, "We checked that one through already
The housekeeper whose place you used called us. Another part
down the street thought he recognized one of Simpson's car
However, Mr. Simpson himself said none of his cars was out an
all his employees were on the premises. A dozen others ca
vouch for it."

"I see."

"Anybody else to back up your side?"

I grinned at him. "I think it can be arranged."

"You're causing a lot of trouble, Mister," he told me.

My grin got big enough so he could see all the teeth. "Hell,
haven't even started yet."

Dari and I drove through town and picked up a macadar
road leading into the hills. Below us to the right Lake Rappah
was a huge silver puddle. Two lesser roads intersected an
joined the one we were on.

At the next bend we came upon the outer defenses of Simp
son's place. A sign read Hillside Manor Private. It was set in
fieldstone wall a good 10 feet high and on top were shards c

oken glass set in concrete. That wasn't all. Five feet out there
as a heavy wire fence with a three-strand barbed wire over-
ng.

"Nice," I said. "He's really in there. How long has it been
e this?"

"Since the war. About '47."

"This guy Simpson . . . he's always had the place?"

"No. There was another. It changed hands about ten years
o. That is, at least the owners changed. But the visitors;
ey're always the same. You never see them in town at all.
hey come and go at night or come in by the North Fork Road
by Otter Pass. Sometimes there are a hundred people up
ere a week or two at a time."

"It can accommodate that many?"

"At least. There are twenty-some rooms in the big house and
x outbuildings with full accommodations. It's almost like a
ige private club."

"Nobody's ever been nosy enough to look inside?"

After a moment she said, "They caught Jake Adler in there
ace and beat him up terribly. Captain Cox has been in a couple
times, but said he saw nothing going on. Several years ago
vo hunters were reported missing in this area. They were
und dead a week later . . . fifty miles away. Their car went
ver a cliff. The police said they had changed their plans and
ecided to hunt elsewhere."

"Could have been."

"Possibly. Only one of them made a phone call from the
otel the day they were supposed to have disappeared."

I looked at her incredulously. "You report that?"

"They said I wasn't positive enough. I only had a photo-
raph to go on and in brush clothes all hunters tend to look
ike."

"Nice. Real nice. How can we get a look in there then?"

"You can see the house from the road a little way up. I don't
now how you can get inside though. The wall goes all the way
round and down to the lake."

"There's an approach on the water?"

Her forehead creased in thought. "There's a landing there
ith a path leading through the woods. It's well hidden in a
nger cove. Are you . . ."

"Let's see the house first."

We found the spot. I parked the car and stood there at the
p, looking across a quarter-mile gulf of densely wooded valley
t the white house that looked like a vacation hotel.

A few figures moved on the lawn and a few more clustered
n the porch, their dark clothes marking them against the stark
hite of the building.

Behind me, Dari said, "A car is coming."

It was a blue sedan, an expensive job, the two in front indi? cernible in the shadows. But the New York City plate wasn't. wrote the number down and didn't bother putting the pen? back. Another plume of dust was showing around the Ott? Pass intersection and I waited it out. We were back to bla? Caddies again and this one had four men in it and upstate Ne? York plates. Fifteen minutes later a white Buick station wag? rolled past and the guy beside the driver was looking my way.

Harry Adrano hadn't changed much in the five years he h? been up the river. His face was still set in a perpetual scowl, st? blue-black with beard, his mouth a hard slash. And Harry w? another number in a crazy combination because wherever Har? went one of the poppy derivatives was sure to follow.

Very softly I said, "Like Apalachin . . . I got to get insi? there."

"You can't. The main gate is guarded."

"There's the lake . . ."

"Somebody will be there, too. Why do you have to go inside?

"Because I want to get the numbers on any cars that are u? there."

"You'll get killed in there."

"You know a better way?"

The smile she gave me matched her eyes. "Yes. Grac? Shaefer was in town yesterday. She'll be making herself avai? able for the . . . festivities there."

"Do you think she'll go along with that?"

Dari's smile changed. "I figure you'll be able to coax her int? it."

"Thanks," I said.

I took her arm and headed for the car. Before we reached it ? heard tires digging into the road up ahead and tried to duck bac? into the brush. It wasn't any good. The black Cad swept b? going back toward town and both the guys in it had plenty ? time to spot the two of us, if they had bothered to look. ? didn't seem that they had, but Benny Quick was driving an? that little punk could see all around him without moving h? head.

We waited, heard the car fade off downhill, then got in th? truck. At the Otter Pass turn-off, fresh tire tracks scarred th? dirt and a broken whiskey bottle glinted at the side of the road?

Just beyond the North Fork Road, the road turned sharply? and that's where they were waiting. The Cad was broadside t? us and Benny was standing beside it. If we were just casua? tourists, it would look like a minor accident, but anything els? and it was a neat trap.

I braked to a stop 20 feet short of the Caddy and stuck m?

92

head half out the window so the corner post covered most of my face. Benny Quick tried to adjust a pleasant smile to fit his squirrely expression, but did a lousy job of it.

But Benny wasn't the one I was worried about. Someplace nearby the other guy was staked out and there was a good chance he had a rod in his fist. I tugged the .45 out and thumbed the hammer back. Beside me Dari froze.

I put on the neighborly act, too. "Trouble, friend?"

Benny started toward me. I opened the door of the cab and swung it out as if I were trying to get a better look. I saw Benny take in the Willie Elkins' Garage, Repairs and Towing Call Pinewood 101 sign printed there, make a snap decision, figure us for locals in the woods, and decide to write us off as coincidence.

His smile stretched a little. "No, . . . no trouble. Pulled a little hard on the turn and skidded around. Just didn't want anybody ramming me while I turned around."

He got in the Cad, gunned the engine, and made a big production of jockeying around in the small area. He wound up pointing back toward the mountain and waved as he went by. I waved too and at that moment our eyes met and something seemed to go sour with Benny Quick's grin.

Either he was turning it off as a bad fit a little too fast or he recognized me from a time not so long ago.

Around the bend ahead I stopped suddenly, cut the engine, and listened. Then I heard a door slam and knew Benny had picked up his passenger. Dari was watching me and I didn't have to tell her what had just happened.

Silently, her eyes dropped to the .45 on the seat, then came back to mine. She said, "You would have killed him, wouldn't you?"

"It would have been a pleasure," I said.

"It's terrible," she whispered.

"Well, don't let it snow you, kid. I may have to do it yet."

It was dark when we reached the hotel. The clerk waved Dari over and said, "Right after you left a call came in. Girl said she was Ruth Gleason. She sounded almost hysterical. I couldn't make much out of it. She was crying and talking about needing somebody."

Dari's face turned ashen. She turned to me, waiting. "You said you could reach Grace Shaefer," I reminded her.

Dari nodded.

"See if she can meet us at Jimmie's bar in an hour."

Ten minutes went by before the operator got my call through to Artie. As usual, we made idle talk before I gave him the plate numbers I had picked up on the mountain road. He grunted disgustedly when I told him I wanted it right away. This would take a little time, so I left the number of the hotel and said I'd stand by.

I looked at my watch and told the clerk to put any calls through to me in Dari's room.

Dari's room was on the ground floor at the end of the corridor. I knocked and heard her call for me to come in. I stood there a moment in the semidarkness of the small foyer and then, unlike her, turned the key in the lock. Inside I could hear her talking over the phone.

She was curled up on the end of a studio couch, wrapped in a black and red mandarin robe that had a huge golden dragon embroidered on it. The fanged mouth was at her throat.

She had a Mrs. Finney on the wire. Trying to conceal her annoyance, Dari said, "Well, when Grace does call, can you have her meet me at Jimmie's in an hour? Tell her it's very important. All right. Thanks, Mrs. Finney."

She hung up and grimaced. "She knows where Grace is, damn it."

"Why is it a secret?"

"Because . . ." she gave me an impish grin, "Mrs. Finney's rooming house is . . . a little more than a rooming house. During the summer, that is."

"Oh," I said. "And she's still loyal to her . . . clients?"

"Something like that."

"The national pastime. No place is too big or too little for it. Any town, anyplace, and there's always a Mrs. Finney. Do you think she'll speak to Grace?"

"She'll be there." She stood up, the satiny folds of the robe whipping around her until the golden dragon seemed almost alive.

There is some crazy fascination about a big woman. And when I looked at her I knew that her love was my kind, greedy, wanting to have everything; violent, wanting to give everything. Her eyes seemed to slant up and the front of the robe followed the concavity of her belly as she sucked in her breath. Her breasts were high and firm, their movement making the dragon's head move toward her throat hungrily.

I held out my hand and without hesitation she took it. When I pulled her toward me she came effortlessly, sliding down beside me, leaning back against the cushions with eyes half-slitted to match those of the guardian golden dragon.

My hands slid around her, feeling the heat of her body through the sheen of the satin. There was nothing soft about her. She was hard and vibrant, quivering under my touch and, although she was waiting, she was tensing to spring, too, and I

94

uld sense the flexing and rolling of the muscles at her stomach
d across her back.

Her fingertips were on me, touching with wary gentleness and
aving the knowledge of possession, but first exploring the full-
ss of something she now owned. One hand went behind my
ead, kneaded my neck, and the other guided my face to hers.
o word was spoken. There was need for none. This was the
ow when everything was known and everything that was to be
ould be.

She held me away an instant, searching my face, then, realizing
ow we both desperately hated the silent restraint, did as a
oman might and licked my lips with her tongue until they were
s wet as her own and with a startled cry let herself explode into
kiss with me that was a wild maelstrom of a minute that
emed to go on endlessly.

My fingers bit into her wrists. "Now you know."

"Now I know," she answered. "It never happened to me
efore, Kelly."

Dari raised my hands to her mouth, kissed the backs of my
ands and smiled.

"What do we do now?" she asked me.

"We don't throw this away, kid. It's ours. We'll take it right
nd keep it forever."

Slowly she uncoiled, stood in front of me and let all the love
n her face tell me I had said what she wanted to hear but didn't
xpect.

She let me watch her, then laughed deep in her throat and
aid, "What are you thinking?"

"I'm thinking that you're not wearing anything at all under
hat . . . geisha thing."

"You're right," she said.

She let me look and hunger another moment, then fingered the
lasp of the robe. She held each edge in her hand and threw her
rms back slowly, unfolding the robe like immense, startlingly
rimson wings, and stood outlined against them in sheer sun-
anned beauty highlighted by the mouth so red and hair so
londe.

With another smile my Valkyrie turned and moved away
lowly into the bedroom opposite, and behind me the phone
ang so suddenly I jumped.

The desk clerk said, "Mr. Smith, I have your New York call."

My tone stopped Artie's usual kidding around.

"Okay, buddy," he said, "but you got yourself a mixed-up
ackage. Two of those cars, a station wagon and a sedan, belong
o businessmen who show clean all the way."

"Maybe, Art, but Harry Adrano was riding in the wagon and
hat boy's been working with the happy dust."

95

"That one Cadillac is a rented car. The guy who signed out for it is a Walter Cramer nobody knows anything about, but the guy who paid the tab *is* something. He's Sergei Rudinoff, Soviet attaché who's been in this country three months."

I thanked Art, hung up, and stared at the phone. The picture was coming through loud and clear.

Dari took me out back to her car and handed me the keys.

It was 8:30. Jimmie spotted us when we walked in and came down.

"Grace Shaefer's in the back. Said she's waiting for you."

I grinned back and we headed for the back room.

Grace Shaefer sat there nursing a highball. She was a wide eyed brunette with a voluptuously full body in no way disguised by the black, low-cut dress. The white swell of her breasts was deliberately flaunted, the outline of her crossed legs purposely apparent. One time she had been beautiful, but now her beauty had gone down the channels of whoredom.

"Hello, Dari. Who's your big friend?"

"This is Kelly Smith. How have you been, Grace?"

Her smile was to me, a plain invitation, though she spoke to Dari. "I've been fine. Let's say, I have everything I've ever wanted."

"Grace . . . are you going up on the hill this time?"

"Yes, I am," she said, almost defiantly. "Why?"

Before Dari could answer I said, "How thick are you involved, Grace?"

"Say, look . . ."

"You're hooked, baby. You can get out of it if you want to."

There was genuine fear in her eyes. "I got the feeling you're looking to get yourself killed," she told me.

"It's been tried. Now . . . how about you? If you want, you can do me a favor up there."

When she answered I knew she had made up her mind. She said, "Smithy boy, like you know my kind, I know yours. Let's not turn our backs on ourselves. The day I want to commit suicide I'll do you a favor, otherwise from now on stay clear of me. That plain?"

I nodded. But Grace wasn't finished yet. With that subtle intuition some people have, she knew what was between us and said to Dari, "I could do you a favor though, Dari. Mr. Simpson is having a party tonight. He could do with more girls. One thing a pretty bitch like you can be sure of, you'll always be welcome up there. Just come willingly. Remember?"

I grabbed Dari's arm before she could hit her and with a de

liberate smirk Grace tossed her furs over her shoulders and walked out.

The outside door slammed open. The kid who came in was scared and out of breath. He gasped and said, "Mr. Smith . . ."

Then I recognized him. Sonny Holmes, the one who braced Paley and Weaver in the bar over the Evans girl.

"Mr. Smith . . . they're looking for you. I'm telling you, they're after you bad."

I grabbed his shoulder. "Who?"

"Those two you fought with because of me. They were over at your hotel asking for you and the desk clerk said you'd be here."

"Those two don't bother me."

"Maybe not them, but they went outside and talked to some others in a car. A Cadillac from the hill."

"Benny Quick spotted me. That little bastard finally got his memory back. Well, the next time I tag him he won't have any memory left." My voice came through my teeth.

"Mr. Smith, you better get out of here."

Without knowing it, I had the .45 in my hand.

"Look, kid, you take Miss Dahl out of here. Get in her car and make sure you're not followed. Try to get to the police. You tell Cox his town is about to explode."

"No, Kelly . . ."

"Don't start bugging me now, Dari. Do what you're told. This is my kind of business and I'll take care of it my way."

She glanced at the gun. "That's what I'm afraid of. Kelly . . . don't let's spoil it so quickly, please, Kelly." She paused, her eyes wet. "You've been one of them. I think everybody knew it. You carry a gun . . . you've been shot . . . you're here in the middle of all this. Run, darling . . . please. I don't care what you were, don't stay part of this or they'll kill you!"

"Not while I have a rod, kitten."

Her words sounded flat. "That's just as bad, isn't it?" she asked. "You kill them . . . and the law kills you."

I could feel the amazement in the short laugh I let out. I cut it off, grinned, and handed her the .45. "Okay, kitten, have it your way."

She dropped the gun in her pocket, went to kiss me, and then everything out in the bar went quiet. Before she could move, I shoved her in Sonny's arms and whispered harshly, "Take her, damn it!"

When the door closed behind them I turned, ran to the bank of windows at the side of the room, and felt for the catch. Slowly, a drop of sweat trickled down my back. The windows were the steel casement awning type and somebody had removed the crank handles. Another second and they'd be back here and there wasn't time to break out.

At the end of the room were the johns and on a sudden thought I turned into the one marked WOMEN. If they searched the place they'd go to the other one first instinctively. There was no lock on the outside door, but a waste basket fitted under the knob. Another couple of seconds maybe. The window there was the same as the others, steel casement with the handle gone. It was shoulder high and the opaque, wire-impregnated glass was practically unbreakable.

Outside, I heard muffled voices. I cursed softly, fighting the stem of the window handle. It wouldn't budge. I reached back, grabbed a handful of paper, and wrapped a section around the toothed edges. This time when I twisted, the stem gave a little. With exasperating slowness the window began to swing out. On the other side of the wall a heavy foot kicked the door open and somebody said, "Come on out of there!"

If the men's room was the same as this, they could see the shut window and know I didn't go out it, but they couldn't see into the closed toilet booth and would figure I was holed up there. I grinned, thinking that it was a hell of a place to be trapped.

The window was out far enough then. I hauled myself up, squirmed through the opening as a hand tried the door.

Under me was a driveway. One end was blocked by a building, the other was open into the lighted street. I ran toward the light and was a second too late because somebody cut the corner sharply and I could see the gun in his fist.

But the edge was still mine. He had not yet adjusted to the deep black of the alley, and for me he was a lovely silhouette. He could hear my feet and raised the gun. Before he could pull the trigger I crossed one into his jaw that took bone and teeth with it and he hit the ground as if he were dead and I spilled on my face across him.

The other guy was on top of me before I could get up. I dove for the gun the first guy had dropped, fumbled it, and the other one had me.

He should have shot me and been done with it. Instead he cut loose with a running kick that seemed to splinter into my bad side like I had lain on a grenade. It was the amazing agony of the kick that saved me. I arched away from the next one with a tremendous burst of energy and my spasmodic kick spilled the guy on top of me.

I had the other gun then. Grabbing it was instinctive. Slamming it against his ear was instinctive.

Never before had the bulging fire in my side been like this, not even when it happened. I tried to wish myself unconscious . . .

98

anything to get away from it. And instinctively I realized
that the only thing that would stop it was up in my room at the
hotel.

Then it's over and you don't know how it happened. You
don't remember the route, the obstacles, the staircase. You can
almost forget instinct as you open the door, then it's there again,
because the door should have been locked and you throw yourself on the floor as a little bright flash of light winks in the darkness. Getting the gun up is instinctive and as something tugs into
the flesh of your upper arm you put out the light that has been
trying to kill you.

A few feet away something crumples to the floor and you get
up, flip the switch, and see Benny Quick lying face up with a
hole between his eyes.

I didn't waste time. I shook out six capsules and washed them
down. For a minute I stood there, waiting for the relief to
come. And gently it came, like a wave of soft warm water, so
that once more I could think and act like a person instead of an
instinct-led animal.

They were looking for me on the street. They'd come here
next to check with Benny. They'd find Benny dead and the big
hunt would be on. My mind was fuzzy now. I shoved the gun
under my belt, stuck Benny's in my pocket, and got my hands
under his arms. Benny had died quickly. A scatter rug covered
the signs of his final exit and I dragged him outside, closing the
door after me.

I could think of only one place to put him. I got him down the
back stairs and around the corner to the door of Dari's room. I
dragged the body in and dumped it on the floor because it was
as far as I could go with it.

Across the room a girl was trying to scream. She watched me
with eyes so black they seemed unreal and when she got done
trying to scream she collapsed on the floor.

The girl began to sob. I knew who she was. Tentatively, I
said, "Ruth? Ruth Gleason?"

She seemed to realize that I wouldn't hurt her. The glazed
look left her eyes and she got her feet under her. "Y-yes."

"Dari . . . have you see Dari?"

"No . . . I tried to . . . I waited . . ."

Think, I thought, *damn it, THINK!*

The Holmes kid would have taken her somewhere. Dr.
McKeever had the Evans girl at his wife's sister's place. The kid
would go there.

"Would you know Dr. McKeever's wife . . . or her sister?" I
asked.

For a second Ruth Gleason stopped being scared and bobbed her head, puzzled. "Her sister is Emma Cox . . . Captain Cox's wife. They . . . don't live together anymore."

"Can you drive?"

She nodded again. I reached in my pocket and threw her the truck keys. "Willie Elkin's truck. It's out back. You call Doctor McKeever and tell him to meet us at his sister's. You'll have to drive."

I could hear her voice but couldn't concentrate on it. I felt her hand on my arm and knew I was in the truck. I could smell the night air and sometimes think and cursed myself mentally for having gone overboard with those damned capsules.

Time had no meaning at all. I heard Dr. McKeever and Dari and felt hands in the hole in my side and knew pieces of flesh were being cut away from the hole in my arm. There was Dari crying and the Gleason girl screaming.

All she could say was, "You're a doctor, give it to me, please. You have to! Oh, please . . . I'll do anything . . . please!"

Dari said, "Can you . . . ?"

There were other voices and McKeever finally said, "It'll help. Not much, but it will quiet her."

"And Kelly?" she asked.

"He'll be all right. I'll have to report this gunshot wound."

"No." There was a soft final note in her voice. "He has to get away."

Ruth Gleason was crying out for Lennie to please come get her.

The pain-killing fog I was wrapped in detached me from the scene then.

"You've been withdrawing, haven't you, Ruth?" Dr. McKeever asked.

Her voice was resigned. "I didn't want to. Lennie . . . took it away. He wanted to . . . get rid of me."

After a moment McKeever continued, "When did it start, Ruth?"

Her voice sounded real distant. "On the hill. Flori and I . . . went there. Flori needed the money . . . her father . . ."

"Yes, I know about that. What about you?"

"A man . . . before Lennie. We met downtown and he . . . invited me. It sounded like fun. He gave me some pot."

Dari said, "What?"

"Marihuana," the doctor told her. "Then what, Ruth?"

"Later we popped one. For kicks. Week later."

"Flori, too?"

Ruth giggled. "Sure," she said, "everybody. It was fun. We danced. Nude, you know? No clothes. Mr. Simpson came in and watched. He gave me five hundred dollars, can you imagine? Flori too. And that was only the first time. Oh, we did lots of dances. We wore costumes for Mr. Simpson and we made his friends laugh and we . . ."

You could barely hear her voice. "Mr. Simpson wanted . . . something special. On different nights . . . he'd take one of us. He made us undress . . . and he had whips. He said . . . it wouldn't hurt." She almost choked, remembering. "I screamed and tried to get away, but I couldn't!" She buried her face in her hands.

"You went back, Ruth?"

"I . . . had to. The money. It was always there. Then there was Lennie. Then I had to because . . . my supply was gone . . . I needed a shot bad. I . . . what's going to happen to me?"

"You'll be taken care of, Ruth. Tell me something . . . are any girls up there now?"

"Yes . . . yes. The ones who are usually there. But there will be more. Mr. Simpson likes . . . new ones. Please . . . you'll have to let me go back."

The voices were miles away now. Sleep was pressing down on me and I couldn't fight it off.

It was daylight. I cursed and yelled for somebody and the door opened and McKeever was trying to push me back on the cot. Behind him was Sonny Holmes.

I managed to sit up against the pressure of McKeever's hand. My mouth was dry and cottony, my head pounding. A tight band of wide tape was wound around my torso and the pain in my side was a dull throbbing, but it was worse than the hole in the fleshy part of my arm.

"I haven't seen anything like you since the war," McKeever said.

From the door Cox said, "Can he talk?"

Before McKeever could stop me I said, "I can talk, Captain. Come on in."

Cox's arrogant smile was gone now. Like everybody else in Pinewood, he had a nervous mouth.

I said, "I made you big trouble, boy, didn't I?"

"You had no right . . ."

"Tough. You checked my prints through, didn't you?"

He couldn't hide the fear in his eyes. McKeever was watching me too now. "I'm a federal agent, laddie, and you know it. At any time my department has authority to operate anywhere and by now you know with what cooperation, don't you?"

Cox didn't answer. He was watching his whole little world come tumbling down around him.

"You let a town run dirty, Cox. You let a worm get in a long time ago and eat itself into a monster. The worm got too big, so you tried to ignore it and you played a mutual game of Let Alone. It outgrew you, buddy. I bet you've known that for a long, long time. Me happening along was just an accident, but it would have caught up to you before long anyway."

Cox still wouldn't put his head down. "What should I do," he asked.

I got up on the edge of the bed, reached for my pants, and pulled them on. Somebody had washed my shirt. Luckily, I could slide my feet into my moccasins without bending down.

I looked hard at the big cop. "You'll do nothing," I said. "You'll go back to your office and wait there until I call and tell you what to do. Now get out of here."

We both watched Cox shuffle out. His head was down a little now. McKeever said, "Can you tell me?"

I nodded. "I have to. If anything happens to me, you'll have to pass it on. Now I'm going to guess, but it won't be wild. That big house on the hill is a front, a meeting place for the grand brotherhood of the poppy.

"It isn't the only one they have . . . it's probably just a local chapter. It's existed, operated, and been successful for . . . is it ten years now? Down here, the people maybe even suspected. But who wants to play with mob boys? It wouldn't take much to shut mouths up down here. To make it even better, that bunch spread the loot around. Even the dolls could be hooked into the action and nobody would really beef. Fear and money were a powerful deterrent. Besides, who could they beef to? A cop scared to lose his job? And other cops scared of him?

"But one day the situation changed. Overseas imports of narcotics had been belted by our agencies and the brotherhood was hurting. But timed just right was the Cuban deal and those slobs on the hill got taken in by the Reds who saw a way of injecting a poison into this country while they built up their own machine. So Cuba became a collection point for China-grown narcotics. There's a supposedly clean businessman up there on the hill who owns an airline in Florida. The connection clear?"

I grinned, my teeth tight. "There's an even bigger one there, a Russian attaché. He'll be the one who knows where and when the big delivery will be made. There's a rallying of key personnel who have to come out of hiding in order to attend a conclave of big wheels and determine short-range policy.

"It's a chance they have to take. You can't be in the business they're in without expecting to take a chance sooner or later. Lack of coincidence can eliminate chance. Coincidence can provide it. I was the coincidence. Only there was another ele-nent involved . . . a Mr. Simpson and his peculiar pleasures. If he had forgone those, chance never would have occurred."

It was a lot of talk. It took too damn much out of me. I said, "Where's Dari?"

The doctor was hesitant until I grabbed his arm. When he looked up his face was drained of color. "She went after Ruth."

My fingers tightened and he winced. "I put Ruth . . . to bed. What I gave her didn't hold. She got up and left. The next morning, Dari left too."

"What are you talking about . . . *the next morning?*"

"You took a big dosage, son. That was yesterday. You've been out all this time."

It was like being hit in the stomach.

I stood up and pulled on my jacket.

The doctor said, "They're all over town. They're waiting for you."

"Good," I said. "Where's Sonny Holmes?"

"In the kitchen."

From Sonny's face, I knew he had heard everything we had said. I asked him, "You know how to get to the lake without going through town?"

Sonny had changed. He seemed older. "There's a way. We can take the old icecart trail to the lake."

I grinned at the doctor and handed him a card, "Call that number and ask for Artie. You tell him the whole thing, but tell him to get his tail up here in a hurry. I'm going to cut Dari out of this deal, doc." The look on his face stopped me.

"She's gone," he said. "She went up there as guest. . . . She said something about Ruth Gleason saying they wanted girls. She had a gun in her pocketbook. She said it was yours. Kelly . . . she went up there to kill Simpson! She went alone. She said she knew how she could do it . . ."

And that was a whole day ago.

Sonny was waiting. We used his car. My rented truck was gone. Ruth Gleason had taken it and the silenced gun I had used was in it.

Mort Steiger said, "I was waiting for you."

"No fishing, pop," I told him.

"I know what you're going to do. I knew it all along. Somebody had to. You looked like the only one who could and who wanted to."

I turned to Sonny. "Call the doc, kid. See if he got through to my friend."

Mort held out his hand and stopped him. "No use trying.

The phones are all out. The jeep from the hill run into a pole down by the station and it'll be two days before a repair crew gets here."

"Sonny," I said, "you get back to Captain Cox. You tell him I'm going inside and to get there with all he has. Tell him they're my orders."

Mort spit out the stub of a cigar. "I figured you right, I did. You're a cop, ain't you?"

I looked at him and grinned. My boat was still there where I had left it. The sun was sinking.

The guy on the dock died easily and quietly. He tried to go for his gun when he saw me and I took him with one sudden stroke. The one at the end in the neat gray suit who looked so incongruous holding a shotgun went just as easily.

An eighth of a mile ahead, the roof of the house showed above the trees. When I reached the main building I went in through the back. It was dark enough now so that I could take advantage of shadows. Above me the house was brilliantly lit. There was noise and laughter and the sound of music and women's voices and the heavier voices of men.

There could only be a single direct line to the target. I nailed a girl in toreador pants trying to get ice out of the freezer. She had been around a long time, maybe not in years, but in time you can't measure on a calendar. She knew she was standing an inch from dying and when I said, "Where is Simpson?" she didn't try to cry out or lie or anything else.

She simply said, "The top floor," and waited for what she knew I'd do to her. I sat her in a chair, her feet tucked under her. For an hour she'd be that way, passed out to any who noticed her.

It was another 20 minutes before I had the complete layout of the downstairs.

What got me was the atmosphere of the place. It was too damn gay. It took a while, but I finally got it. The work had been done, the decisions made, and now it was time to relax.

My stomach went cold and I was afraid of what I was going to find.

It didn't take any time to reach the top floor. Up here you couldn't hear the voices nor get the heavy smell of cigar smoke. I stood on the landing looking toward the far end where the corridor opened on to two doors. To the left could be only small rooms because the corridor was so near the side of the building. To the right, I thought, must be almost a duplicate of the big room downstairs.

And there I was. What could I do about it? Nothing.

The gun in my back said nothing.

Lennie Weaver said, "Hello, jerk."

Behind Lennie somebody said, "Who is he, Len?"

"A small-time punk who's been trying to get ahead in the business for quite a while now. He didn't know what he was bucking." The gun nudged me again. "Keep going, punk. Last door on your left. You open it, you go in, you move easy, or that's it."

The guy said, "What's he doing here?"

I heard Lennie laugh. "He's nuts. Remember what he pulled on Nat and me? They'll try anything to get big time. He's the fink who ran with Benny Quick and turned him in to the fuzz."

We came to the door and went inside and stood there until the tremendously fat man at the desk finished writing. When he looked up, Lennie said, "Mr. Simpson, here's the guy who was causing all the trouble in town."

And there was Mr. Simpson. Mr. Simpson who only went as far as his middle name in this operation. Mr. Simpson by his right name, everybody would know. They would remember the recent election conventions or recall the five percenters and the political scandals a regime ago. Hell, everybody would know Mr. Simpson by his whole name.

The fleshy moon face was blank. The eyes blinked and the mouth said, "You know who he is?"

"Sure." Lennie's laugh was grating. "Al Braddock. Like Benny Quick said, he picked up something some place and tried to build into it. He wouldn't have sounded off, Mr. Simpson. He'd want any in with us for himself. Besides, who'd play along? They know what happens.

"What shall we do with him, Mr. Simpson?" Lennie asked.

Simpson almost smiled. "Why just kill him, Lennie," he said and went back to the account book.

It was to be a quiet affair, my death. My hands were tied behind me and I was walked to the yard behind the building.

"Why does a punk like you want in for?" Lennie asked. "How come you treat life the way you do?"

"The dame, pal," I said. "I got a yen for a dame."

"Who?" His voice was unbelieving.

"Dari Dahl. She inside?"

"You are crazy, buddy," he told me. "Real nuts. In ten minutes that beautiful broad of yours goes into her act and when she's done she'll never be the same. She'll make a cool grand up there, but man, she's had it. I know the kind it makes and the kind it breaks. That mouse of yours won't have enough spunk left to puke when she walks out of there." He laughed again. "If she walks. She may get a ride back to the lights, if she wants to avoid her friends. A guy up there is willing to take second smacks on her anytime."

"Too bad," I said. "If it's over, it's over. Like your two friends down at the lake."

Lennie said, "What?"

"I knocked off two guys by the lake."

The little guy got the point quickly. "Hell, he didn't come in over the wall, Len. He came by the path. Jeeze, if the boss knows about that, he'll fry. The whole end is open, if he's right."

But Lennie wasn't going to be taken. "Knock it off, Moe. We'll find out. We'll go down that way. If he's right or wrong, we'll still fix him. Hell, it could even be fun. We'll drown the bastard."

"You watch it, Len; this guy's smart."

"Not with two guns in his back and his hands tied, he's not." His mouth twisted. "Walk, punk."

Time, time. Any time, every time. Time was life. Time was Dari. If you had time, you could think and plan and move.

Then time was bought for me.

From somewhere in the darkness Ruth Gleason came running, saying, "Lennie, Lennie . . . don't do this to me, please!" and threw herself at the guy.

He mouthed a curse and I heard him hit her, an open-handed smash that knocked her into the grass. "Damn these whores, you can't get them off your back!"

Ruth sobbed, tried to get up, her words nearly inaudible. "Please Lennie . . . they won't give me . . . anything. They laughed and . . . threw me out."

I just stood there. Any move I made would get me a bullet so I just stood there. I could see Ruth get to her feet and stagger, her body shaking. She held on to a stick she had picked up. I could see the tears on her cheeks.

"Lennie . . . I'll do anything. Anything. Please . . . you said you loved me. Tell them to get me a fix."

Lennie said two words.

They were his last.

With unexpected suddenness she ran at him, that stick in her hands, and I saw her lunge forward with it and the thing sink into Lennie's middle like a broken sword and heard his horrible rattle. It snapped in her hands with a foot of it inside him and he fell, dying, while she clawed at him with maniacal frenzy.

The other guy ran for her, tried to pull her off, and forgot about me. My hands were tied. My feet weren't. It took only three kicks to kill him.

Ruth still beat at the body, not realizing Lennie was dead.

"Ruth . . . I can get you a fix!" I said.

The words stopped her. She looked at me, not quite seeing me. "You can?"

"Untie me. Hurry."

I turned around and felt her fingers fumble with the knots at my wrists until they fell free.

"Now . . . you'll get me a fix? Please?"

I nodded and hit her. Later she could get her fix. Maybe he'd made it so she'd never need one again. Later was lots of things, but she'd bought my time for me and I wouldn't forget her.

The little guy's gun was a .32 and I didn't want it. I liked Lennie's .45 better, and it fitted my hand like a glove. My forefinger found the familiar notch in the butt and I knew I had my own gun back and knew the full implication of Lennie's words about Dari.

She had tried for her kill and missed. Somebody else got the gun and Dari was to get the payoff.

This time I thought it out. I knew how I had to work it. I walked another 100 yards to the body of the gray-suited guard I had left earlier, took his shotgun from the ground and four extra shells from his pocket, and started back to the house.

Nothing had changed. Downstairs they were still drinking and laughing, still secure.

I found the 1,500-gallon fuel tank above ground as I expected, broke the half-inch copper tubing, and let the oil run into the whiskey bottles I culled from the refuse dump. It didn't take too many trips to wet down the bushes around the house. They were already season-dried, the leaves crisp. A huge puddle had run out from the line, following the contour of the hill and running down the drive to the front of the house.

It was all I needed. I took two bottles, filled them, and tore off a hunk of my shirt tail for a wick. Those bottles would make a high flash-point Molotov cocktail, if I could keep them lit. The secret lay in a long wick so the fuel oil, spilling out, wouldn't douse the flame. Not as good as gasoline, but it would do.

Then I was ready.

Nothing fast. The normal things are reassuring. I coughed, sniffed, and reached the landing at the first floor. When the man there saw me he tried to call out and died before he could. The other one was just as unsuspecting. He died just as easily. Soft neck.

Mr. Simpson's office was empty. I opened his window, lit my wick on the whiskey bottle, and threw it down. Below me there was a small breaking of glass, a tiny flame that grew. I drew back from the window.

I had three more quarts of fuel oil under my arm. I let it run

out at the two big doors opposite Simpson's office and soak in
the carpet. This one caught quickly, a sheet of flame coming c
the floor. Nobody was coming out that door.

Some place below there was a yell, then a scream. I opened th
window and got out on the top of the second floor porch roo
From there the top floor was blanked out completely. Heav
drapes covered the windows and, though several were open fo
ventilation, not a streak of light shone through.

I stepped between the window and the draperies, entirel
concealed, then held the folds of the heavy velvet back. It was
small theatre in the round. There was a person shrouded i
black tapping drums and that was all the music they had. Tw
more in black tights with masked faces were circling about
table. They each held long thin whips, and whenever th
drummer raised the tempo they snapped them, and sometime
simply brought them against the floor so that the metal tip
made a sharp popping sound.

She was there in the middle, tied to the table. She was robe
in a great swath of silk.

From where I stood I could see the town and the long line o
lights winding with tantalizing slowness toward the hill.

Down below they were yelling now, their voices frantic, bu
here in this room nobody was listening. They were watching th
performance, in each one's hand a slim length of belt that coul
bring joy to minds who had tried everything else and nov
needed this.

She was conscious. Tied and gagged, but she could know wha
was happening. She faced the ring of them and saw the curtai
move where I was. I took the big chance and moved it enough s
she alone could see me standing there and when she jerked he
head to keep anyone from seeing the hope in her eyes I knew i
was the time.

There was only one other door in the room, a single door o
the other side. It was against all fire regulations and now they'
know why. I lit the wick on the last bottle, let it catch hold all th
way, stepped inside, and threw it across the room.

Everything seemed to come at once . . . the screams, th
yelling from outside. Somebody shouted and opened the big
doors at the head of the room and a sheet of flame leaped in or
the draft.

There was Harry Adrano. I shot him.

There was Calvin Bock. I shot him.

There was Sergei Rudinoff. I shot him and took the briefcase
off his body and knew that what I had done would upset the
Soviet world.

There was the man who owned the airlines and I shot him.

Only Nat Paley saw me and tried to go for his gun. All the

rest were screaming and trying to go through the maze of flame at the door. But it was like Nat to go for his gun so I shot him, too, but not as cleanly as the rest. He could burn the rest of the way.

I got Dari out of the straps that held her down, carried her to the one window that offered escape, and shoved her out. In the room the bongo drummer went screaming through the wall of flame. From far off came staccato bursts of gunfire and now no matter what happened, it was won.

I shoved her on the roof and, although everything else was flame, this one place was still empty and cool.

And while she waited for me there, I stepped back inside the room, the shrivelling heat beating at my face, and saw the gross Mr. Simpson still alive, trapped by his own obesity, a foul thing on a ridiculous throne, still in his robes, still clutching his belt . . .

And I did him a favor. I said, "So long, Senator."

I brought the shotgun up and let him look all the way into that great black eye and then blew his head off.

It was an easy jump to the ground. I caught her. We walked away.

Tomorrow there would be strange events, strange people, and a new national policy.

But now Dari was looking at me, her eyes loving, her mouth wanting, her mind a turbulence of fear because she thought I was part of it all and didn't know I was a cop, and I had all the time in the world to tell her true.

THE AFFAIR WITH THE DRAGON LADY

THE AFFAIR WITH THE DRAGON LADY

Now that that wise guy photographer from *Life* found us out there's hardly any sense making up excuses for what happened. We might sound like a pack of idiots to some, but, damn it all, for two whole years we had a lot of fun with our secret society and crazy clubhouse and in a way it's a shame to see it all end.

Only watch out who you call crazy, because you'd be surprised at the big names who put on the *Dragon Lady* costume for one of the meetings and tucked same costume away in a locked trunk in the attic and hoped for another invite back.

Like all good things, though, it had to come to an end. And, like most good things, it took a dame and a calamity to bring it about, so now our secret society is out in the open where all can see it and to save wear and tear on the tarmac I'll tell you about it.

The story really starts back in October of '45 and you know how that was. All of us coming out of the service all at once with a pocket full of dough, if you were lucky, and plenty of places to spend it. If you were lucky enough to be married, you settled down right away. If you weren't, you made all the places, saw all the faces, joined the 52-20 club until you got a job, and from then on wondered what had happened to three or four years and didn't know whether to be sad or glad about being in civvies.

Well, there we were, the 10 husbands of the *Dragon Lady*. Our mutual wife was a B-17E with bullet-hole acne, a patched-up tail, and joints that creaked and groaned even when she was trying to rest. Still, she was a thing of beauty who took us all there and back 82 times, twice almost giving her own life in a grand gesture that we might live, but survived because our love for her was just as strong.

You can imagine having to leave her. We each took a little piece of her away in our B-4 bags, kissed her mutilated body, and left her there with tears of 100 octane dripping from No. 1 and No. 4 engines. Don't ever tell us an airplane can't cry.

We did, too, because, behind us, strangers took her to a far away prison in the desert with others of her kind, put her in solitary confinement behind plastic shrouds and left her there to die in whatever strange way airplanes are supposed to die.

Us? We all came home to the same state, settled down within three counties of each other and began the slow disintegrating process of living. We all wrote, sent greeting cards, got drunk, and went phone happy sometimes, but we stayed in touch. From Ed Parcey, the tail gunner, up to me as first pilot, we all had babies a few times, named them after each other until you could hardly tell who from whom on the roster.

That is, all of us except Vern Tice, our old co-pilot who out and out refused to enter the marital state because he didn't want to get like us. Which is to say, weathered out of our own desires by women who made better mothers than wives and wanted the same thing from both children and husbands alike.

Hell, it's an old story, why repeat it?

Charlie Cross, our engineer, and I wanted to operate a rice-seeding outfit using Stearmans. The wives cried us out of it. Henry Lucerne, the navigator, Vic Cabot, the radioman, and "Tiny" Sinkwich, who handled the right waist gun, were going to patent and manufacture an electronic homing device for private planes.

That meant a few initial hardships, the giving up of minor, but stable, positions and the women sulked them out of that. Needless to say, somebody else invented and sold the same thing and made a fortune, but when you mentioned it to the girls you only got a frosty stare.

Lou Kubitsky, the other waist gunner, didn't do too badly. Before the war he was a fighter and, had he gone back into it, he would have had his head knocked off. Instead, he became a grocer and, when the community developed, his store was in the center of it and he made out just great. He was happy, all right, but he sure hated groceries. So on the side he managed a couple of fighters, sparred with them and kept his hand in.

George Poe, Arnie Castle and Fred Halloway were salesmen for the same firm of Coster and Selig, Printers, lived in the same northeast sector of the suburbs, borrowed each other's tools, and looked to the sky whenever a prop job went over, and studiously ignored the blow jobs as interlopers. Each had a wife who had sweated out all 82 missions and to whom even talk of flying was anathema.

So there we were, all paramours of the *Dragon Lady*, and, with one exception, no longer bold, but getting old. And when that lone exception showed up it meant a lot of fun for a while as long as you could take a week of cold silences, too-casual meals, and a few other things pouting women can conjure up.

Which brings us back to Vern Tice again.

He was 38 last year, still in good shape with hardly any gray showing and no sign of fat, good looking as always, with a mint in his back pocket he had picked up on speculative deals most smart money stayed away from. His big deal was banking a Broadway show for 50 per cent that gave him a gigantic return with a year and a half run. But women? Oh, he loved 'em all. Marry one? After seeing the trap we were all in?

Laugh, laugh.

That's the way things stood the day old Vern blew in driving
white Jag with the leading lady of *Fielder's Choice* next to him.
he was a big blonde beaut dripping diamonds and furs with a
ugh like ice clinking in a highball and without her as a come-on
e never would have made the briefing because it was an axiom
mong the women that we should never all get together at the
ame time.

Elaine Hood fixed that. Every one of the girls wanted a look
t this fabulous creature who was all over the covers of current
magazines and in most of the gossip columns every week. Smart
oy, that Vern. He had checked her out well on her procedures,
nen let her solo in this strange world of suburbanism.

One thing about her. She was ready for combat right off. She
idn't go into it with her head up and locked, not a bit. That
irl had all her guns armed and went into tactical maneuvers
ke a 50-mission vet. The other women never had a chance,
eally.

So after supper at the country club they were all glad to let
ne boys go hang around the bar for once while they started
umping Elaine for all the latest tidbits.

Being Monday, we had the bar all to ourselves, toasted the old
ays a few times, then Charlie Cross said with peculiar feeling,
"To the old girl herself. To the *Dragon Lady*, laddies."

We lifted our glasses to that one, all right.

When we put them down Vern said, "Miss her, don't
ou?"

"Come off it," George Poe said, "who doesn't? Man, I've put
n a thousand missions in dreams since I saw her last."

"How'd you all like to see her again?" Vern said.

For a good 10 seconds it was real quiet. If anybody else had
aid that there would have been the usual good natured groans
of acknowledgment, but this time it was Vern who said it and
suddenly we knew what the pitch was. We *knew*, but we couldn't
be quite sure.

Tiny Sinkwich turned around real slowly and put up some
ack-ack. "She's long gone in some smelter's pot, buddy. That
or blown up doing drone duty for rocket jockeys in F-100s."

Vern's grin went all the way across his face. "You think?"

I said, "Okay, kid, drop your flaps and take us in. You've had
something cooking ever since you taxied up. Now start de-
briefing."

He was enjoying every second of it. He had us hanging by
our shroud lines and wasn't cutting us loose until he had to.
Finally he said, "I bought the *Dragon Lady*."

"*You what?*" Charlie's voice was almost a squeak.

"That's right. I bought her. I went through surplus sales and
dragged the old girl out of the pile and right now she's sitting

over at the Lakemore Airfield in the big hangar as pretty as yo[u] please."

"You're crazy," I said, "Lakemore's abandoned. It's [a] swamp from where the water backed up from the governme[nt] dam project. You couldn't put a Piper Cub in there."

Vern grinned again and nodded sagely. "I know. She went [in] by truck."

From down at the end where Ed Parcy guarded the tail out [of] sheer force of habit, he said skeptically, "There's no road in[to] there, buddy."

Between sips of his drink Vern said, "There is now. I boug[ht] a road, too. Those steel mats they used to lay up for temporar[y] runways over sand or muck. Worked real well."

"Lakemore Airfield was owned by . . ." Vic Cabot started [to] say.

Then Vern cut him off with, "The Blakenship family. [I] bought it from them. The deed is free and clear and all ours.[

I think we said it all at once. "*Ours?*"

He laughed at the expressions on our faces. "Sure. Yo[u] don't think I'd keep the old dame all to myself, do you?"

Henry Lucerne said, "But . . ."

"Look," Vern told all of us. "I've watched you guys losin[g] your lift ever since we left the *Lady*. You're all like kids wi[th] your toy taken away and those dames in there . . ." he waved [a] thumb over his shoulder, "won't give it back. Well, now the[y] got trouble because we got our dame back and she's all ours."

You don't say much at a moment like that. You try to think [of] something but it won't come out so you have a drink to cove[r] your astonishment and when it's down it all begins to mak[e] sense. Everybody tried to talk at once, slap each other's back an[d] finally came to the same thought.

They left it up to me to put it into words. I said, "There['s] only one problem, friend. We can't fly her around. It woul[d] cost an arm and a leg for fuel and parts—and who knows if w[e] can even get her license back?"

"So who needs to fly?" Vern asked me.

I just looked at him. In fact, we all did.

He laughed and said, "Buddies, we got ourselves the crazie[st] clubhouse anybody ever saw on the best patch of ground f[or] fishing and duck shooting in the whole state."

And when we thought about it, he was right.

Thus began the second saga of the *Dragon Lady*.

Elaine Hood was a real pro at her job. She hinted that if th[e] gals "could only" take off a week she'd like to show them aroun[d] the big town north of us and you never saw nine wives go t[o] work so fast. Oh, we let them sweat a little bit and work thei[r] female wiles to the limit, but finally we okayed their flight plans[.]

116

let them arrange for in-law baby sitters, and saw them all off at the station.

That same day we all started our vacations and went back to our true love, our one wife, the *Dragon Lady*, and there behind the faded and weather-worn walls of the old hangar primped and petted her until she was a thing of beauty again.

A flip of a switch would bring her to life for us. She would quiver when you touched the controls, talk to you when you pressed the mike button, and through some almost forgotten G.I. genius we could warm her belly in winter and cool it in summer.

Since we were lovers and not fighters any more, it was appropriate to redesign the *Lady*, but she didn't mind. In fact, she seemed to welcome the change. She liked the addition of the bar and the compact gas range and oversize refrigerator. The tables and chairs fitted in just right and the TV set seemed to have always belonged there.

Oh, we kept her in character. No gaudy paint jobs when we had cans of o.d. around. Outside on her skin we tickled her with brushes and brightened up the original markings. A few of the old wounds needed to be sutured up once more and she was all the better for it.

In one week we had her laughing again and a dozen week-ends later she was ours, all ours, to love and cherish as we wished. Ah, what a second honeymoon we had! It took a lot of tailoring to get into our wedding clothes again, but we got the uniforms back on, the mold off the leather, and the film off the brass.

I'm glad *Life* didn't see us then, coming out of the old tool shed that we made into a dressing room, turned out in old AAF pinks and greens and dress khakis. We saluted each other silly, patted the surplus chutes that hung from hooks under our names and slipped into the hangar under blackout conditions like back in England when we knew Jerry was upstairs looking for a target.

When the door was closed, Tiny said, "Everybody in?"

A murmur went around our heads, sounding strangely hollow in the vault of the hangar.

"Okay," Tiny said. "Flip 'er."

Vern pulled the switch, flooded the place with lights placed just so and for all the world we were back there on the stand waiting for take-off.

"Beautiful," somebody said, "just beautiful."

And in the same order, just like back in '44, we climbed aboard the *Dragon Lady* to celebrate our wedding night all over again, bringing to her gifts to show our love . . . the same little bits and pieces we had all taken away as mementos years before, gently put them back where they belonged . . . and the night was consummated in grand style.

Now that was the beginning. You can only keep a beauty like the *Lady* quiet for so long. A man just has to brag, and having done so, has to back up his talk and before long the *Dragon Lady* had an entourage the way any royal dame should. Of course, only ex-AAF personnel were invited to a "flight" on that Baker One Seven, and even then they had to conform to spec. Orders of the day said you went on board in the appropriate uniform and those who didn't have one, either borrowed Class As or dug up something in surplus.

You can bet one thing. Nobody was ever disappointed. Before long that old hangar became a lavish combination Officers' and N.C.Os' Club where men could be men in the old style, fight the war as they pleased, and forget the crazy old world outside. It was the place of the Permanent Pass, the Big Open Post, the Fabulous Furlough.

Nobody was old there. When they felt that way they could find their places inside the *Dragon Lady* and she would console them within herself and give them back their youth.

Of course, Vern Tice knew what he was doing all the time. The place was paying off in grand style and, although the fees were small, all the money stayed in the barracks and finally we had a bomber base to beat all bomber bases. Never was one staffed so adequately with so much rank and so many sergeants.

Never was the location of one base so carefully guarded.

Oh, those women on the home front knew something was going on, that's for sure. They'd beg and wheedle to find out what it was, but what man in his right mind is going to give his wife the address of his mistress?

Now right here I have to mention that there was *one* woman who knew the score. That was Elaine Hood, who by now had become big in Hollywood—picked up an Oscar, but didn't pick up Vern Tice no matter how hard she tried, and believe me she tried.

Vern didn't know it, but all of us married pigeons knew it. Those already trapped can look back and see the pitfalls.

One thing you have to say about old Elaine. She never squealed. She knew all about our mistress and could have let out the big secret to the town at any time. Good kid, that one, no chicken any more, but still lovely and with a complete sense of understanding. She became good friends with all the wives of the *Lady*'s original crew and sort of welded them together to the point where they began liking each other's company and

ould even stand for hangar talk over the supper table at the
ountry club.

In fact (and we say it was because they were afraid to compete
ith the *Dragon Lady*), they even helped when Tiny, Vic and
Henry pooled all their savings and started making electronic
quipment. Lou Kubitsky sold his store, opened a sports arena,
nd made a bundle. Irene, his wife, sold tickets and loved it.
Come to think of it, things like that were happening to every-
ody.

And back at the Happy Hangar way out there in the swamps,
he fishing grew better, the duck shooting greater, and all the
tate would have wanted in on it had they known it was there.
But it was our secret and none would give it away. Vern made
is like he always did, but he wasn't so happy about it any more.
You could tell. When the flight was over and the crew left for
heir bunks, Vern would take off in his Jag and go prowling
round. Sometimes he'd go see Elaine, but when he came back
ou could see he was having a struggle with himself and it took
 hard mouth to tell some of the women to lay off the match-
making attempts and let him and Elaine be. If the guy didn't
vant to get married, so let him live in a BOQ.

It was about then, at the end of summer, that two things
happened simultaneously. Elaine finished her run on Broadway and the Air Force decided to reactivate Ellison Field,
bout 10 miles out of town. So Elaine moved into an apartment
n Avery Road around the corner from us and the 332nd moved
o F-100's into Ellison.

Those great big air-borne hogs overhead made all the kids
happy and brought smiles to the faces of merchants, but to
us old prop men they were just noise makers that needed too
damn much runway to get off and 10 times that to get back
down.

But they raised hell with our hangar hours because whenever
one of those blow jobs would go by overhead it made our *Dragon
Lady* seem suddenly old and that was one thing we just couldn't
tolerate. It got so that when we saw one of those pink-cheeked
pilots on the street we'd freeze him down, him in his blues that
made him look like he never got out of the kaydets.

Maybe if it hadn't been for the Vern Tice-Elaine Hood side-
line show we all would have had pilot fatigue, but those two
were flying the craziest kind of sidewalk formations you ever
saw. Everybody but Vern knew it was love, but, even if he did
know, she was the enemy to be avoided. He enjoyed the combat
angle, the boy-girl stuff, but when it came to the Big Tangle, he
put his nose down and hit for the barn.

My wife was the one who put her finger on it. Vern had th[e] old gang back together again and he was afraid that marriage t[o] Elaine would be like bailing out on the return leg of a milk run She'd have him off in Hollywood or back on Broadway and n[o] even a goodbye kiss for his true lady fair in the hangar, and th[at] he couldn't stand.

It was right in the middle of the fall that everything came to [a] head. Vern and Elaine finally had it out and, from what [I] heard by way of eavesdropping on a phone conversation, sh[e] was going back to Hollywood to do a picture and Vern was goin[g] to stay put. I passed the word around because by now we wer[e] all on her side and hated to see Vern a permanent party in th[e] BOQ when he could just as easily get married.

He claimed it was just a case of misery wanting company, bu[t] I knew that he was talking through his hat even if he didn[t] admit it. And that was the way things stood the night of ou[r] anniversary party. The whole squadron had assembled to chee[r] up Vern, damn the interlopers at Ellison Field, and drink to ou[r] ever-loving mistress, the *Dragon Lady* who was the fairest [of] them all, bar none, no none at all.

Ah, yes, this was to be a night! Waldo Casey and the Stephan[s] brothers had brought along six converts between them and, lik[e] all first timers, they had bad gaposis in their old uniforms. Yo[u] never did see guys have so much fun, though.

Yeah, we were really rolling along about 8, hangar flying a[s] usual, winning the war personally, turning all the little thing[s] into big things.

Upstairs a jet cracked the sound barrier with one hell of [a] bash and for a few seconds everyone stopped talking.

Maybe it was a half-hour later that the phone rang and afte[r] Tiny answered it he edged up to Vern who was talking to me an[d] said, "It's for you, Vern."

Now nobody but nobody outside our own group has tha[t] number and this night everybody was here. That left Elain[e] I watched Vern get grim around his mouth and he shook hi[s] head just once. "Tell her nix, Tiny."

Then Tiny shook his head. "Not me, buddy. She said yo[u] speak to her because this one's important. She made it stick too."

Vern frowned a little bit. "How?"

"Brother," Tiny said, "can she use G.I. language. You bette[r] talk to her."

Vern frowned at that, shrugged, and picked up the phon[e] took a breath and said, "All right, chick, what's up?"

It came out real funny because the phone was hooked up to [a] speaker system like we used to have overseas and it let the worl[d] in on the know.

Elaine came back so sharp and quick it was like she was trying to bite him. "One of the kids from Ellison just went down."

"So let the Air Force take care of their own. They're autonomous now."

Without being asked to, all the talk came to a standstill. It was as if they were waiting for the bomb to drop, not knowing whether to stay there or run for it.

"Listen, you knothead," she said, "look at the wings you're wearing."

Everybody there looked down at his own chest.

"Those wings he's got on are the same as yours even if they are a whole generation younger. He's one of your own. Do you understand that?"

"Well, what can we . . ."

"He ejected over that damn swamp you playboys call home. He's down right in the middle of it some place and he could possibly be hurt."

"Okay, okay, sugar, but what am I supposed to do?"

"Do? *Do something!* You've been fighting that war so long the only thing you have out there are heroes and you ought to be able to think of something. You're officers, aren't you? You're enlisted specialists, aren't you? Maybe you can take that damn crate of yours and . . ."

"All right, baby, hold it there. You're coming over loud and clear only don't run the old girl down. Where are you?"

"At Ellison with the boy's wife. They live next door to me."

"Where at Ellison?"

"On the flight line," the speaker said. Her voice was flatter now.

"Okay, baby, now calm down. Is there any way there you can contact base ops?"

"I'll find a way."

"Good, then you call from there and by then we'll have something ready."

She hung the phone up almost before he finished and when we looked around it was like looking at the bunch about to hit Ploesti. For a moment the heroes were gone and they were butchers, bakers and candlestick makers again, slightly paunchy, a lot balder, a little bewildered from being civilians so long. And then Vern spoke.

"Gentlemen," he said. That was all. They all edged in close and the heroes were back once more. They wore the damndest grins you ever did see and every hat went over at a jauntier angle and they were ready. *And I mean ready.*

"We're in a peculiar position here. I dare say we are the only ones alive who know that swamp area. It's relatively new, so there are no old timers on it."

I heard Jonesy laugh and say, "Hell, I made a lot of daw
patrols after bass, man."

"I know," Vern told him, "but there's no moon tonight."

Henry Lucerne, our old navigator, said, "We'll go, bucky. Ju
hand us the poop from group."

Right then the phone rang. Elaine got her message across fas
because she had literally busted into ops and the C.O. was on he
back. We could hear him squawking over the speaker and the
Pappy Thompson, who managed the big A & P store and wh
had been a general during the war—with the kind of a voice
general should have—reached for the phone and told Vern, "I'
take it."

When he told Elaine to put the C.O. on the guy came on
strong until old Pappy said, "This is General Thompson from
the Four Hundred and Thirteenth."

Now the 413th went out with the war, but that C.O. didn'
know that and he wasn't about to argue with a general.

Pappy said, "What equipment have you there? An
choppers?"

"Er, yes, Sir. Just one, but she's redlined."

"Well dammit, you un-redline it and get it ready. I'll give yo
thirty minutes to have it on the ramp. You got that?"

"Yessir, yessir," the C.O. stammered uncertainly. "But Sir
where are you?"

"With my men, in the swamp where that boy went down
that's where. Now you get every available man ready. Stan
by on an open line and that girl there can pass the messages t
you. I want you to relay them directly. Do you hear? Direct
ly. I want no misunderstanding. No garbled orders. Is tha
clear?"

Well the message went across, all right. You could hear tha
C.O. sounding off on the other end of that line and now it wa
up to us. Nobody bothered to change clothes. The flatboats the
sportsmen used were all drawn up at the edge of the water an
in five minutes were loaded with gear.

They went out three and four to a boat, some paddling and
some with trolling motors. Up front would be one man with a
light and another standing by with a boathook to fend off anything from low hanging branches to cottonmouths.

Vern gave a list of things to Pappy and he called them out to
Elaine. Ambulance, medics, ropes, power saws and a dozen
other things. She'd relay them across the room and the C.O.
would repeat the list.

On the other side of the room the radio that had been drowned
out in the chatter was heard again, and this time it was a special
bulletin. Nobody could figure it out, but with usual Air Force
efficiency an entire rescue team led personally by a general

self was down in the swamps already searching for the lost

r.

We grinned at that, but a sad grin, because we all knew that
a way it was the end of us.

But how that Elaine and Vern did act as a team! You'd think
y had been practicing for this all their lives. We sent Curly
son and Harry Stamph out to direct the crash crews coming
because without a guide they'd never have made it. Even
n we had to use a dozen more to line the road ahead of them
they could pick out the mat under their headlights. Long
grass had grown through the perforations in the steel and
u could hardly tell roadbed from swamp.

You know, it must have been funny to those Air Force boys.
ke having a dream. There we'd be, officers and enlisted
rsonnel side by side working hand in glove, decked out in
iforms that disappeared years back. Something like suddenly
ding yourself in a lost world.

The fly boys who came in on the crash trucks let their mouths
ng open when they dug our 50 mission crushes and the medals
t backed our wings up under the lapels almost. But it didn't
t long. The mud and sweat made everybody look alike pretty
on.

A little after 11, Jonesy found the boy near his favorite bass
le. He was hanging from a tree snarled in his shroud lines.
nesy couldn't tell if he were dead or alive. Everyone was quiet
n, until Charlie and Ed got there with another light and
arlie saw the boy move. There was one hell of a shout for
re joy after that.

Then Charlie gave us the bad news. You couldn't make the
scue with a few flashlights and the crash teams had nothing
be used right then. It would take a couple of hours to rig
mething up.

It had to happen. You just know it had to happen.

*In fact, I think she was there just waiting for it to happen all
ng.*

We told Charlie to hold it a minute and got the Air Force
ds to open hangar doors we never thought would ever be
ened again. Then, after Vern told Elaine, "Hold it a minute,
by, because you're going to hear the sweetest love song ever
ng," the two of us got aboard the *Dragon Lady* and went
rough the check list, and when I said, "Start One," Vern hit
e switch.

Yessir, she sure did croon. On all four big ones she sang to us,
en we opened her eyes wide when we turned on the landing
hts and she brightened up the whole swamp.

Oh, how their faces did look when they saw our lady roll out.
guess it was like seeing a live dinosaur to them, because most

didn't want to believe it at all. Right then the *Lady* was a livi
fire-breathing doll working at what she knew best, taking care
her men, and she was going to make this her last and l
biggest.

There were a few of that gang who weren't that young a
from up in the cockpit I saw them take a hasty swipe at ey
that turned misty all of a sudden and I knew that she was th
lady too as much as she was ours.

Vern went back to the phone and Pappy got the tail jacked
and somehow they were able to swivel our girl around so th
midnight was turned into noon, and all the while those fo
big engines turned generators by whose light a life was bei
saved.

They got out there with the power saws, cut their w
through to the kid in the tree, roped the debris back with winch
lined up along the shore, but it wasn't quite enough.

It took the chopper to get him out. Vern directed him in, th
Charlie Cross and Ed got the kid in a sling along with a med
who got out there and like it all started . . . suddenly . . . it w
all over. Almost, anyway. We put the *Lady* back to sleep, but s
wasn't quite the same. She was mired to her belly in the mu
of the swamp, but we all kissed her tenderly, even those pin
faced Air Force kids, and the two older guys who did it rath
forcefully and seemed reluctant to leave her, then we all went
the hangar to smash the glasses in the fireplace. The war w
over.

Well, that's when that *Life* photographer found us. Don't a
me how he got there, but he had popped pictures all over t
place and there we were, two generations apart, drinking to t
old girl outside. Yeah, it made quite a story, our secret society
B-17 lovers who had some harmless good times like it was sti
long time ago.

And, of course, now we had to let the girls in, but you c
believe it's no sewing circle setup because this is a man's cl
where all you have to do to get rid of the women is schedule
sex lecture. They don't act up, though. They're all the better f
it. Let them get raunchy and you just wave a finger at the beau
ful doll under colored lights in the background. You don't bu
the *Dragon Lady* in her own house.

Oh, didn't I tell you? That new Air Force over at Ellis
threw us a thankyou party and got our lady back out of t
muck and into a hangar whose interior *really* is decorated wi
some of the most beautiful "salvage" you ever saw.

Vern? Shucks, he and Elaine got married and here's t
kicker. They did the bit right in the hangar and I was the be
man and when she came down the aisle beside the *Dragon La*
he almost keeled over with surprise because instead of a weddi

124

own she was wearing the same thing she wore in '44, the pinks
and greens of an Army nurse and she was a rank over old Vern.

First thing he did after the ceremony was make old Pappy
promote him so he could give her orders. Then he turned and
winked at the *Dragon Lady*.

And I'll be hanged if she didn't wink back!

THE END

A SELECTION OF FINE READING AVAILABLE IN CORGI BOOKS

NOVELS

N7638	GOING TO MEET THE MAN	James Baldwin	5/-
N7335	THE SNOW BALL	Brigid Brophy	3/6
N7637	NINA'S BOOK	Eugene Burdick	5/-
N7317	THE CHINESE ROOM	Vivian Connell	5/-
N 7692	THE TOBACCO MEN	Borden Deal	6/-
N1278	THE GINGER MAN	J. P. Donleavy	5/-
N7488	BOYS AND GIRLS TOGETHER	William Goldman	7/6
N7640	NIGHTMARE COUNTY	Frank Harvey	5/-
N1500	CATCH-22	Joseph Heller	7/6
N095	WHITE LOTUS	John Hersey	7/6
N7656	PINKTOES	Chester Himes	5/-
N7671	A THUNDER AT DAWN	Jack Hoffenberg	7/6
N7193	MOTHERS AND DAUGHTERS	Evan Hunter	7/6
N7675	MONMOUTH HARRY	A. M. Maughan	6/-
N7552	THE BAWDY WIND	Nan Maynard	3/6
N7301	WEEP NOT, MY WANTON	Nan Maynard	5/-
N7351	CARAVANS	James A. Michener	6/-
N7594	HAWAII (colour illus.)	James A. Michener	10/6
N7322	UNTAMED	Helga Moray	5/-
N1066	LOLITA	Vladimir Nabokov	5/-
N7683	THE BIG LAUGH	John O'Hara	5/-
N7684	ELIZABETH APPLETON	John O'Hara	5/-
N7685	THE HORSE KNOWS THE WAY	John O'Hara	7/6
N1162	A STONE FOR DANNY FISHER	Harold Robbins	5/-
N7642	BROTHER SURGEONS	Garet Rogers	6/-
N7655	THE HONEY BADGER	Robert Ruark	7/6
N7670	HOW I WON THE WAR	Patrick Ryan	5/-
N7641	THE LONG VALLEY	John Steinbeck	3/6
N7661	THE RED PONY	John Steinbeck	3/6
N7578	THE DEVIL IN BUCKS COUNTY	Edmund Schiddel	7/6
N7567	THE DEVIL'S SUMMER	Edmund Schiddel	7/6
N7600	THE RUNNING FOXES	Joyce Stranger	3/6
N1133	THE CARETAKERS	Dariel Telfer	5/-
N7352	EXODUS	Leon Uris	7/6
N7517	WIND FROM THE CAROLINAS	Robert Wilder	7/6
N7674	WAIT FOR TOMORROW	Robert Wilder	6/-
N7672	SQUIRREL'S CAGE	Godfrey Winn	3/6
N7690	THE UNEQUAL CONFLICT	Godfrey Winn	5/-
N7116	FOREVER AMBER Vol. I	Kathleen Winsor	5/-
N7117	FOREVER AMBER Vol. II	Kathleen Winsor	5/-
N7689	THE CZAR	Thomas Wiseman	7/6

WAR

B7695	THE HOLOCAUST KINGDOM	Alexander Donat	6/-
B7622	THE GREAT WAR AT SEA (illustrated)	A. A. Hoehling	7/6
B7375	THE DESTRUCTION OF DRESDEN (illustrated)	David Irving	6/-
B7494	THE MARE'S NEST	David Irving	6/-
B7691	THE LONG WHITE NIGHT	Eric Lambert	3/6
B7557	THE SECRETS OF D-DAY	Gilles Perrault	5/-
B7290	POPSKI'S PRIVATE ARMY	Vladimir Peniakoff	7/6
B7635	TOBRUK	Peter Rabe	5/-
B7476	THE SCOURGE OF THE SWASTIKA (illustrated)	Lord Russell of Liverpool	5/-
B7477	THE KNIGHTS OF BUSHIDO (illus.)	Lord Russell of Liverpool	5/-
B7703	THE DEATHMAKERS	Glen Sire	5/-

ROMANCE

GR7666	A HOUSE FOR SISTER MARY	Lucilla Andrews	3/6
GR7667	THE FIRST YEAR	Lucilla Andrews	3/6
GR7681	COME BE MY GUEST	Elizabeth Cadell	3/6
GR7701	NIGHT'S DAUGHTERS	Bess Norton	3/6

GOTHIC NOVELS

GR7591	MAULEVER HALL	Jane Aiken Hodge	4/-
GR7576	DARK ENCHANTMENT	Dorothy Macardle	4/-
GR7649	THE HOUSE ON THE FEN	Claire Rayner	4/-

SCIENCE FICTION

HORROR

GENERAL

WESTERNS

CRIME

All these great books are available at your local bookshop or newsagent, or can be ordered direct from the publisher. Just tick the titles you want and fill in the form below.

——————————————————————————————————————

CORGI BOOKS, Cash Sales Dept., Bashley Road, London, N.W.10
Please send cheque or postal order. No currency, PLEASE. Allow 6d.
per book to cover the cost of postage on orders of less than 6 books

NAME ....

ADDRESS ....

(JULY 67) ....